FOR GRANDMA'S SAKE

Chad frowned. "This is serious," he said. "We don't want to make Grandma sick."

Stevie thought about that for a second. It would be terrible if their behavior endangered Grandma Lake's health. And she was only here for two weeks. The least her grandchildren could do was make her stay as pleasant and soothing as possible. "You're right, Chad," Stevie said. "We've got to be on our best behavior. All of us," she added, shooting a glance at Alex. "No pranks or practical jokes."

"No revenge plots," Chad said.

"No horsing around," Alex put in.

Stevie shot him another look, suspicious at his choice of words. But he spread his hands apologetically.

"Sorry," he said. "You know what I mean. We have to act civilized and stuff, like Mom and Dad were saying earlier."

"So for two weeks, all we have to do is act like good, quiet kids and not fight with each other, right?" Michael said.

Stevie nodded firmly. "It won't be easy," she said, "but we have no choice. Grandma's life may depend on it."

THE SADDLE CLUB #73

HORSE GUEST

BONNIE BRYANT

A SKYLARK BOOK
NEW YORK · TORONTO · LONDON · SYDNEY · AUCKLAND

RL 5, 009–012

HORSE GUEST

A Bantam Skylark Book / January 1998

ISBN 0-553-48623-3

Published simultaneously in the United States and Canada.

Bantam Books are published by Bantam Books, a division of Bantam Doubleday Dell
Publishing Group, Inc. Its trademark, consisting of the words "Bantam Books" and
the portrayal of a rooster, is Registered in U.S. Patent and Trademark Office and in
other countries. Marca Registrada. Bantam Books, 1540 Broadway, New York, New
York 10036.

PRINTED IN THE UNITED STATES OF AMERICA

OPM   0 9 8 7 6 5 4 3 2 1

*I would like to express my special thanks
to Catherine Hapka for her help
in the writing of this book.*

"HE DID IT again," Stevie Lake said, peering over the half door into the stall.

Lisa Atwood sighed. Carole Hanson just shook her head in dismay and opened the stall door. The horse inside, a big chestnut gelding named Magoo, rolled his eyes at her and snorted. He shifted his weight nervously from leg to leg, but he didn't move. That was because he had managed to get a pile of the stall's straw bedding built up between his legs.

"If we had given him a few more hours in there, he wouldn't have been able to move at all," Lisa commented.

"Hold him still for a second, will you?" Carole said. "I'll

get some of this straw out of the way, and then we'll take him out and put him in cross-ties in the aisle. That will make it easier to work on him."

The three girls set to work. Being best friends, they didn't have to talk much to work together perfectly as a team. Lisa stepped forward and slipped a halter onto the horse's head. Then she held him while Carole pushed some of the straw out from under his belly. Carole was careful to keep one hand on the horse's side to let him know where she was. Magoo was by nature a nervous and easily startled horse, and she didn't want him to get scared and kick her.

Meanwhile, Stevie was in the aisle, unpacking the bucket that contained Magoo's first aid and grooming kit. "Do you think we should hot soak his foot again today?" she asked as Lisa led Magoo into the aisle and cross-tied him.

"It can't hurt," Carole said. She glanced critically at Magoo's slightly swollen left foreleg. "Judy says it's not getting better as quickly as she'd like."

Judy Barker was the equine vet who treated the horses at Pine Hollow Stables. Pine Hollow was where Carole, Stevie, and Lisa rode. It was also where the three girls had decided to form The Saddle Club, which had only two rules: Members had to be horse-crazy and they had to be willing to help each other out. The three founding members of the club had been talking to Judy a lot lately. That was because of Magoo. It was early January, and the girls would be going back to school in a little more than a week. But in the meantime, their winter vacation had been more exciting than usual. That was also at least partly because of Magoo.

On New Year's Eve, The Saddle Club had volunteered to baby-sit for Max Regnery, the owner and manager of Pine Hollow, and Deborah, his wife. The couple had a seven-month-old baby girl named Maxi. While they were baby-sitting, the three friends had received a frantic phone call from Hedgerow Farms, a stable about ten miles away. The roof of Hedgerow's stable building had collapsed, and horses were trapped inside. The Saddle Club had rushed to help, taking Maxi with them, and with Elaine, Hedgerow's manager, they had saved all the horses and brought them to Pine Hollow. Most of the horses had escaped with hardly a scratch. But not Magoo. He had sustained all sorts of injuries. None of them were life-threatening, but because there were so many and because the patient was known to be difficult, Judy had advised leaving Magoo at Pine Hollow until he got a little better. The Saddle Club had volunteered to nurse him, but they hadn't realized quite how big a job they were taking on.

"Bruised sole," Lisa said, beginning a list of Magoo's medical problems as her friends crouched down and carefully checked the horse's foreleg. "Capped hock. Broken knee." She paused. "That last one always sounds so awful."

Carole glanced up, looking surprised. "But Lisa," she

said, "a broken knee isn't like a broken leg. It doesn't mean that the bones in the knee are actually fractured. It just means that the skin is broken on the—"

"I know, I know," Lisa said, holding up a hand. "I don't need one of your famous lectures, Carole."

All three girls laughed at that. Carole was well known for launching into lengthy, detailed monologues on horse care or riding at the least provocation. The lectures were almost always interesting—Carole really knew what she was talking about—but the timing wasn't always appropriate. For instance, at the moment The Saddle Club had a lot of work to do with Magoo. What they needed was less talk and more action.

"I'll go fill a tub with hot water," Stevie volunteered, heading down the aisle.

Carole was examining the gelding's bandages. Several of the ones on his sides and forelegs were frayed around the edges or hanging loose. A couple were gone altogether.

"He's still fussing with his bandages," Carole said, bending closer to peer at an uncovered wound. There were a few specks of straw and dirt embedded in it already. She sighed. "We've got to figure out how to stop him. Otherwise we'll never be able to keep these wounds from getting infected."

Magoo had turned his head to see what Carole was doing. He snorted and tried to move away from her probing fingers.

4

"It's okay, boy," Lisa said soothingly, going to the horse's head. "We're here to help. Even if you don't seem to believe it." She rolled her eyes at Carole. "Who could have guessed Magoo would turn out to be such a problem patient?"

Before Carole could answer, Stevie reappeared with the tub. She added some Epsom salts to the hot water, then helped her friends convince Magoo to put his injured foot into it. The horse seemed suspicious at first. He lowered his head toward the water, then jerked his leg away as Carole tried to lift it. Eventually, after several tries, the girls succeeded in getting his hoof into the tub.

"It feels good, doesn't it?" Stevie said to the gelding as he relaxed a little. "If you could just remember that from day to day, we wouldn't have so much trouble."

While Magoo's foot soaked, The Saddle Club set to work cleaning his wounds with an antibiotic and replacing the bandages. As they worked, they talked.

"I can't believe the gymkhana is next Saturday already," Lisa said. In December, Max had announced that the first big event of the new year at Pine Hollow would be an informal horse show known as a gymkhana. All the young riders at the stable would divide into teams of four to compete in all sorts of fun and exciting games and races that would test the skills they had been practicing in their riding classes.

Stevie looked up from her examination of the scabby wound on Magoo's right knee. "I can't believe we haven't come up with any good ideas for events yet," she said, sounding a little grumpy.

Carole and Lisa exchanged glances. They knew that when Stevie said "we," she was really referring mostly to herself. Stevie had a quick and amazingly creative mind. She was famous for inventing interesting and original ideas for gymkhana games. But this time she hadn't managed to come up with a single one yet.

"Don't feel bad, Stevie," Lisa comforted her. "We've been a little busy lately."

Stevie didn't look comforted. "I mean, practically everybody else has given Max tons of ideas for wacky games," she said. "Adam came up with an ice-cream-sundae-making race." She frowned. "That one should have been mine."

Carole laughed. "True," she said. "And what about Polly's idea for a backward obstacle course? That one will really be challenging." Adam Levine and Polly Giacomin were both in The Saddle Club's riding class.

"That's a good one," Lisa agreed. "But can you believe that even Veronica diAngelo came up with a good idea?" Veronica was The Saddle Club's least favorite person at Pine Hollow. Her family was extremely wealthy, and Veronica thought that made her better than everybody else. She took a lot more pride in her expensive wardrobe than in her riding skills, although she was a better-than-average rider in spite of that. Her horse, a blue-blooded champion named Danny, had cost more than Carole's horse, Starlight, and Stevie's horse, Belle, put together.

Stevie made a face at the mention of Veronica's name. "It figures her game has to do with shopping," she said. "It's her favorite activity." Veronica had suggested a race in which players had to match merchandise with the correct receipts and then return them to the right "store" to win. Max had seemed a little doubtful, but he had agreed to add the game to the gymkhana as long as Veronica promised to supply the props.

"There's still a week until the gymkhana," Carole told Stevie, reaching for a clean bandage. "I'm sure we can come up with some good ideas before then."

"Okay," Stevie said. "Let's start now. I was thinking about doing some kind of race where two riders have to cross the ring together while tossing something back and forth between them."

Lisa grinned. "That sounds hard. But fun."

"What would they throw?" Carole asked. "Tennis balls or something?"

Stevie shrugged. "I hadn't really thought about that," she said. "I guess tennis balls would work. But that seems kind of boring. Maybe we could use ripe tomatoes. Or raw eggs."

"Ugh," Lisa said, picturing egg yolk and tomato innards splattered everywhere. "I'm not sure Max will go for that. This gymkhana is going to be inside, remember?"

"Hmmm," Stevie said. "That's too bad. It would be a lot more fun if the riders had to go back to the starting line if they dropped the ball—or whatever—instead of just chasing it down. Eggs would work perfectly. So would water balloons, I guess. But that's been done to death."

"How about snowballs?" came a soft voice from nearby.

The three girls looked up in surprise. They hadn't realized that anyone was close enough to hear their conversation. A slender girl with reddish brown hair and freckles was standing just a short way down the aisle. She had approached so quietly that The Saddle Club hadn't noticed her until she had spoken. Only Magoo had been aware of the girl's approach. His ears were pricked toward her curiously.

"Oh, hi, Britt," Carole greeted the newcomer.

Stevie didn't bother with greetings. "Snowballs!" she exclaimed. "It's brilliant. Why didn't I think of that?"

The girl just smiled timidly. Brittney Lynn had been coming to Pine Hollow for less than two weeks. She and her mother had just moved to the area, and Britt was riding at the stable on a trial basis. If things worked out, she would become a permanent member of The Saddle Club's riding class.

So far, The Saddle Club could tell that Britt was a very good rider—almost as good as Carole. Other than that, they still didn't know much about her. The new girl was painfully shy, which didn't make getting to know her very easy. But they were trying.

8

"Have you been out on the trail, Britt?" Lisa asked. She had just finished rebandaging a gash on Magoo's hind leg, so she stood and stretched her back.

Britt shook her head. "I was riding Diablo in the indoor ring," she said, her voice so soft that Lisa had to lean forward a little to hear her. "Max wanted me to try him out." Since Britt was new to the stable, Max was letting her try several of his horses before deciding which one she would ride in class.

"What did you think of him?" Carole asked. She had ridden Diablo herself in the past, and she knew that he was an appropriate choice for a rider of Britt's ability. But the gelding could be feisty, and Carole wondered if his strong personality might intimidate such a shy girl.

"He's a nice horse," Britt said.

Carole exchanged glances with her friends. Was that really all Britt had to say about Diablo? Now that she stopped to think about it, Carole realized that Britt didn't ever have much to say about anything. If someone had asked Carole what *she* thought of Diablo—or any other horse she'd ever met—her answer could easily have gone on for most of the day. Stevie and Lisa would have been almost as bad.

Britt didn't seem to notice the glances. She was looking at Magoo, who was starting to get fidgety again. "How's he doing?" she asked. Everyone at Pine Hollow knew Magoo's story by now.

That took Carole's mind off of Britt's shyness immediately. "He's a little better," she said. "But not much." She went on to explain exactly why, in quite a bit of detail.

Lisa let her talk for about five minutes while she and Stevie finished cleaning and bandaging Magoo. Then she decided it was time to rescue Britt. "Carole," she said sharply, interrupting a monologue about applying poultices to an infected area, "I think you've already told Britt what she wanted to know."

"And more," Stevie added with a wink at Britt.

Carole stopped talking. For a second, she looked annoyed at the interruption. Then she grinned sheepishly. "Sorry, Britt," she said. "I guess I was getting a little carried away."

"Maybe you should add 'college professor' to your list of possible careers," Stevie suggested. She turned to Britt. "You see, Carole knows she wants to work with horses when she grows up. She's just not sure whether she wants to be a competitive rider, a trainer, a riding instructor, a vet, a breeder—"

"Or all of the above," Lisa finished for her.

Britt looked a little confused. She smiled uncertainly but didn't say anything. There was a moment of awkward silence.

Suddenly Stevie remembered something. She glanced at her watch. "Oops," she said. "I didn't realize how late it was getting. I've got to get home."

"Oh, that's right," Lisa said. "Your grandmother is coming tonight, isn't she?"

Stevie nodded. "We're having an early dinner, then we're all going to meet her plane at the airport." Stevie couldn't wait to see her father's mother again. Grandma Lake had moved from Pennsylvania to Arizona more than five years earlier, and this was her first trip back to the East Coast. She would be staying with Stevie's family for two weeks. "It will be fun having her here," Stevie added with a smile. "I don't remember too much about Grandma—I was kind of young when she moved—but I know I was always crazy about her. So she must be pretty cool, right?"

"I've got to go, too," Britt murmured, slipping away before the other girls could answer. She had almost reached the end of the aisle when someone came barreling around the corner, slamming into her.

"Watch where you're going!" the newcomer exclaimed angrily, glaring at Britt. It was Veronica diAngelo.

Stevie frowned, momentarily forgetting all about her grandmother's arrival. She dropped the rolled bandage she was holding and hurried toward the site of the collision. Britt, rubbing her elbow where Veronica had bumped it, stared wide-eyed at the other girl.

"Why don't you take your own advice, Veronica?" Stevie said angrily. "You're the one who wasn't looking where you were going."

"Mind your own business, Stevie," Veronica said. She glared at Stevie, then turned her angry gaze on Britt. "Just watch it next time. Or else." She stomped down the aisle to Danny's stall, which was right next to Magoo's, and let herself in.

"Sorry about that, Britt," Stevie said, making sure that her voice was loud enough for Veronica to hear from inside Danny's stall. "But don't worry. Most of the people at Pine Hollow aren't that rude and obnoxious."

"It's no big deal," Britt said in a voice that was practically a whisper. "I've got to go." She hurried away.

Stevie was still scowling as she returned to her friends. "Veronica is such a jerk," she muttered. "If we don't watch out, she'll scare Britt away from Pine Hollow for good."

Carole and Lisa weren't paying attention to her. They had hardly noticed the incident. Lisa was at Magoo's head, trying to keep him as still as possible while Carole dabbed red liquid from a small glass bottle onto a few of his bandages.

"What are you doing?" Stevie asked.

Lisa looked up. "Mrs. Reg suggested it," she said. Max's mother, known to one and all only as Mrs. Reg, helped to run the stable, just as she had done when Max's father was alive. She had a lifetime's experience collecting good ideas for taking care of horses, and she was always willing to share them with the young riders at the stable.

Carole held up the bottle so that Stevie could see the label. "We're putting a little hot pepper sauce on the bandages he's been pulling at. The taste should make him leave them alone."

"What a great idea," Stevie said. "My mom did the same thing to keep the cat from eating her houseplants. It worked like a charm."

"Be careful not to get any of it on his skin," Lisa said worriedly, watching as Carole moved on to the bandage on Magoo's knee. "If that stuff gets in his wounds, it will really sting."

Carole just nodded and concentrated on her job. A few minutes later, she was finished. "Okay, that should do it," she announced, screwing the cap back on the bottle and putting it in the grooming bucket. "And if I'm lucky, my dad won't even notice that I swiped a bottle of his favorite super-spicy taco sauce."

The others laughed, then helped return Magoo to his stall. They had already cleaned it and removed some of the straw to avoid another pileup under his belly. The gelding looked around his home carefully, then returned to the front of the stall to watch the girls as they hurried down the aisle.

When they reached the student locker room, Stevie sat down on a bench in front of her cubby and started to change out of her riding boots. Carole and Lisa sat down nearby to keep her company.

"I wonder if Britt likes it here," Lisa mused. "It's hard to tell, isn't it?"

Stevie glanced up. "That's for sure," she said. "I mean, it's hard to believe anyone *wouldn't* like it here. But then again, Veronica could make anyplace look bad. I hope her obnoxious attitude doesn't scare Britt away before she gets to know some of the nice people here." She grinned. "Like us, for instance."

"I know one thing that could help make her happy," Carole said. "Our latest Saddle Club project."

"Definitely," Lisa and Stevie agreed in one voice.

When Britt had first come to tour Pine Hollow with her mother, Ms. Lynn had asked The Saddle Club to help find her daughter a horse. Britt had had her own horse back in Ohio, but he had retired to pasture just before the family's move. Ms. Lynn wanted to surprise Britt if possible, and The Saddle Club had agreed to keep the project a secret. They were planning to arrange for Britt to ride a number of different horses until she found one she really liked, without telling her what was really going on.

"Actually, I was thinking about stopping by Hedgerow Farms tonight," Lisa said. "I have a ballet lesson, and Hedgerow is on the way to the studio. They have so many gorgeous horses—I'm sure we can find the perfect one for her there."

Stevie nodded as she tossed her riding boots into her gym bag. "You may be right," she said. "Although I also wouldn't be surprised if we found Britt's dream horse right here at Pine Hollow." Most of Max's horses were for sale if the right buyer came along. He was always pleased to match a rider to a "perfect" horse.

"We should keep our eyes and ears open for all possibilities," Carole said. "You never know where the right horse is going to turn up. I already asked Judy to let us know if she comes across anything promising among her patients."

Stevie finished pulling on her sneakers, then checked her watch again. "Let's talk more about this later, okay?" she said. She stood up, not bothering to tie her shoes, and quickly yanked on her coat. "Because if I don't get home soon, my parents won't let me near a horse—*any* horse— for a year!"

A LITTLE LATER, Stevie was seated at the dinner table with the rest of her family. That included not only her mother and father, but also her three brothers.

"Hey, Stevie, don't forget," said her younger brother, Michael, "you have to clear the table tonight. Dad made me set it because you were late coming home from your stupid stable."

"No kidding," Stevie snapped, looking up from her green beans. "You only told me that fifty times already, twerp." She had been doing her best to ignore Michael's complaints. She knew he actually preferred setting the table to clearing it. He was only making such a big deal out of it because Stevie had kidnapped his new pet white mice the week before to get back at him for eating all the ice cream one night.

"Stevie," Mrs. Lake said warningly. "Michael. Behave yourselves, please."

Stevie shrugged and kept eating. But Chad, Stevie's

older brother, jumped in. "I don't blame Michael for being mad, Mom," he said. "Stevie's always late when she's out riding her dumb horse. I had to set the table for her at least five times last month."

Stevie sighed and rolled her eyes. Of course Chad would agree. Stevie had wrapped up a box of horse manure and given it to him as a Christmas present, and he still hadn't forgiven her for it. Besides, she had shown his latest girlfriend a photo of him as a five-year-old swimming naked in the Lakes' backyard pool.

"Chad is right," put in Alex, Stevie's twin brother.

That was no surprise to Stevie, either. Recently, Alex had listened in on one of Stevie's private phone conversations with her boyfriend, Phil. To get back at him for that, Stevie had started a chain letter asking people to send him women's underpants—size extra large. He had received the first batch of responses just a couple of days ago.

"You're always telling us we need to learn to be responsible," Alex went on, gazing earnestly at his parents. "But all Stevie ever does is play around at her stable all the time. She's the least responsible person I know."

Stevie dropped her fork and glared at each of her brothers in turn. "Taking care of Belle is a huge responsibility," she said icily. "But I wouldn't expect you three losers to know anything at all about that sort of thing. It's more work than all of you do put together."

Chad rolled his eyes. "Yeah, right," he said. "Shoveling a little manure and then spending hours gabbing with your friends is *sooo* tough."

Alex snorted with laughter. "Right," he said. "And deciding what color ribbons to tie in her horsie's tail is even harder."

"Boys!" Mr. Lake said sharply. "That's enough. Stevie will clear the table tonight to make up for being late. End of discussion."

But Stevie's brothers weren't finished. "Boo hoo," Michael said in a falsetto, pretending to sob. "I'm Stevie Lake, and I have such a hard life. I have to ride my horse all day long."

"It's such a chore," Chad joined in. "Boo hoo. And then I'm forced to have slumber parties with my girlfriends every other night. It's just too much to bear."

That really was too much for Stevie to bear. Without thinking, she grabbed a green bean off her plate and flung it at her older brother. It hit him square in the forehead. Chad retaliated instantly by dunking his hand in his milk glass and flicking white droplets in her direction. Michael giggled and did the same, while Alex recovered the green bean from the floor and dropped it in Stevie's hair.

Mr. and Mrs. Lake both stood up. "Stop it!" Mrs. Lake shouted. "Right this minute!"

The kids froze.

"What do you think you're doing!" Mr. Lake exclaimed, his face flushed with anger. "Your behavior is outrageous! Is this what my mother is coming all these miles to see? My children acting like they were raised by wolves?"

Stevie gulped. Her father sounded really furious. He looked it, too. And her mother didn't appear to be in a much better mood. Too late, Stevie realized that the day of her grandmother's arrival probably wasn't the best time to start a food fight with her brothers at the dinner table. Even if they *had* asked for it.

"Now," Mr. Lake said. His voice was quieter, but still angry. "I hope this will be the last we'll see of this childish behavior—especially for the next two weeks while your grandmother is here. She never let me get away with such nonsense when I was your age, and I don't want her to think your mother and I have completely lost control of our own home. I expect you all to get along like civilized human beings."

"But Dad," Alex started, "Stevie—"

Mr. Lake didn't let him finish. "That goes for all four of you. And I don't want to hear another word about it."

Mrs. Lake nodded in agreement. "And to make sure you realize that we're serious about that," she said, "all four of you will work together to clear up after dinner." She gestured at the spattered milk droplets all over the table. "And all four of you will make sure there's no sign of the mess you've made here by the time we leave to pick up your grandmother."

Hearing the dangerous tone of her voice, none of the kids dared to utter a peep about that.

"IT WAS ALL your fault," Alex muttered sulkily, glaring at Stevie as he dried a platter.

Stevie snorted. "Then why are you three getting punished? Mom and Dad were right there. They obviously thought it was *your* fault."

The four siblings were in the kitchen washing up. Dinner was over, and the elder Lakes were upstairs making sure that the guest room was ready for Grandma Lake's arrival. The family would be leaving in less than half an hour for the airport.

Chad sighed. "Forget it, Alex," he advised his brother. "Mom and Dad are just worked up about Grandma's visit. I'm sure that's why they didn't see the truth, that it was all Stevie's fault."

Stevie started to retort. But then she stopped to think about something. "Hey, you know what?" she said, sloshing a greasy saucepan in the sink. "Mom and Dad *do* seem awfully anxious about this visit. Do you think there's a reason for that?"

Michael looked up from the dishwasher, where he was trying to shove one more plate into the overcrowded rack. "Duh," he said. "Grandma hasn't been here for a long time. What more reason do you want?"

"No, wait a minute," Alex said, shooting Stevie a curious look. "What are you driving at, Stevie?"

Stevie shrugged. "I don't know," she said. "I guess it has been an awful long time since Grandma moved. It's hard to even remember what she's like."

"I know what you mean," Chad said, leaning on the counter. "I mean, we talk to her on the phone on holidays and stuff. But that's not the same as seeing her in person. I know Dad is right, though—I remember that she was always totally in charge when we used to visit her house in Pennsylvania. When she told us to do something, we did it, no questions asked." He grinned. "But I also seem to remember that she hardly ever told us to do anything we didn't want to do anyway. She used to do a lot of cool stuff with us, like taking us places and helping us make up new games. She even rode my dirt bike once."

"I remember that," Stevie said with a laugh, while Alex nodded. "She rode it better than you did." Then she stopped laughing and sighed. "We always had a lot of fun with her back then. But five years is a long time. Just look how much we've all changed in that time. Do you think Grandma has changed a lot, too?"

"I don't know," Alex said. "She is getting older."

"She was always old, wasn't she?" Michael put in, closing the dishwasher. "I don't really remember her when she lived here. But she's got white hair in the pictures she sends at Christmas."

"Yeah, but that doesn't mean anything," Chad said. "She's had white hair for as long as I can remember." He paused. "Still, she did have to move to Arizona because of her health."

Stevie nodded. "I wonder if that's why Mom and Dad got so upset at us tonight. No matter *whose* fault it was," she added quickly. "Maybe Grandma is really old and sickly now, and they're worried that we'll frighten her or wear her out or something."

Alex shrugged. "I doubt it," he said, though he didn't look nearly as certain as his words sounded. "If that was true, Mom and Dad would just come out and tell us."

"Still," Chad said, "whether Mom and Dad want to make a big deal of it or not, maybe it wouldn't hurt for us to cool it while she's here." He chuckled. "For one thing, if Grandma's anything like her old self, she'll kick our behinds if she thinks we're not behaving right."

Stevie nodded in agreement as she handed the last of the freshly washed pans over for drying. Her memories of her grandmother were pretty fuzzy after all this time, but it was still hard to imagine her as old and frail and delicate. Still, it was better to be safe than sorry. Maybe she and her brothers could tone down their usual behavior for a couple of weeks. At least a little.

Lisa called Carole right after dinner. Colonel Hanson, Carole's father, answered the phone and went to get her. Lisa tapped her foot impatiently while she waited. She had already tried Stevie's number, but there was no answer. Then she had remembered that the Lakes were driving to the airport together that evening to pick up their visitor. But Lisa couldn't wait for Stevie's return to share her news. She was too excited.

"Guess what," she said as soon as Carole picked up the phone.

"Hello to you, too," Carole said with a laugh. "Are you turning into Stevie or something?" Usually Stevie was the member of their group most likely to get excited about something and forget about little courtesies like saying hello and identifying herself.

Lisa laughed. "Sorry," she said. "But I've been dying to call you ever since I got home from ballet. I think I've found the perfect horse for Britt!"

"Really?" Carole said.

Lisa thought her friend didn't sound nearly as interested as she should have. "Really," she said. "I stopped at Hedgerow like I planned, and that's when it hit me. They really do have exactly the right horse for her personality and riding ability."

"I wouldn't be so sure about that," Carole said. "I've been doing some thinking about Britt myself. After you and Stevie both left Pine Hollow today, Mrs. Reg asked me to muck out some stalls. And while I was doing that, I realized that the perfect horse for Britt has been right under our noses all along."

Lisa frowned. She hadn't expected this. Once she had made up her mind about Britt's ideal horse, she had expected both her best friends to agree with her. "But wait until you hear which horse I'm talking about," she said. "You'll see what I mean."

"Well, okay," Carole said. "Who is it?"

Lisa shifted the phone receiver to her other ear before answering. "It's that Appaloosa mare," she said. "Applesauce."

"Oh," Carole said. "I see what you mean. She does seem like a pretty good choice." After the girls had rescued the Hedgerow horses, the entire string had spent a few days at Pine Hollow while their new stable was being finished. The Saddle Club had gotten to know most of them pretty well, including Applesauce, a handsome Appaloosa mare with a calm, wise disposition.

"So you agree with me?" Lisa said happily.

"I didn't say that," Carole said. "I think Applesauce would be a good choice. But Coconut is an even better one."

"Coconut?" Lisa repeated. Coconut had been a Pine Hollow school horse for years. He was happy, friendly, polite, and well trained, and Lisa understood immediately why Carole had chosen him. Coconut was talented and spunky enough to challenge a good intermediate rider like Britt, but his temperament was sunny and even, which would keep him from intimidating the shy girl.

"Wouldn't he be great for cheering her up?" Carole prompted. "He's got such a nice personality. And she always seems so solemn and worried. Coconut is just what she needs to help her laugh a little and relax."

Lisa twirled the phone cord around her finger. "I guess so," she said. "But Applesauce has a good personality, too. And she always seems so steady and confident, like she knows exactly what she's doing. Maybe some of that would rub off on Britt and make her more confident, too."

There was a moment of silence as each girl thought about the other's choice. Finally Carole spoke up. "Well, I think either one of those horses could be the one. I'm still voting for Coconut."

"And I'm still voting for Applesauce," Lisa said.

Carole laughed. "Uh-oh. I guess Stevie will have to be the tiebreaker."

Lisa laughed, too. She knew as well as Carole did that the only one who could make the final decision was Britt herself. Only she would know which horse really suited her—whether it was Applesauce, Coconut, or another horse entirely.

"Maybe we can figure out a way to get Britt to try both horses," she said. "If she seems to like one or both of them, we can talk to her mom and see what she wants to do."

"Okay," Carole agreed. "I'll see if I can subtly convince Max that Britt should try riding Coconut tomorrow."

"I'll invite Britt to come with me to Hedgerow sometime soon and visit Applesauce." Lisa smiled. "And may the best horse win."

WHILE HER FRIENDS were talking on the phone, Stevie was sitting in a hard plastic chair at the airport. The plane from Arizona was more than forty-five minutes late, and the entire family was watching for it out the big, glass windows of the waiting room.

Finally they saw a plane taxiing up to the gate.

"Is that it?" Michael asked, yawning and rubbing his eyes sleepily.

25

"I think so," Mr. Lake said. He peered at the plane as it sidled up to the building. "Let's go wait by the gate."

Moments later, the entire family watched as people began to spill through the door of the jetway that had been hooked to the plane. Stevie scanned each face as it emerged. Most looked nothing like the way she remembered her grandmother. There were old faces, young faces, male and female faces. . . . Finally one face appeared that matched Stevie's memories.

"Is that her?" she whispered to her mother.

Before Mrs. Lake could respond, Mr. Lake had rushed forward to greet the white-haired woman. "Mom!" he exclaimed. "Let me help you with those bags."

Grandma Lake relinquished them gratefully. "Thanks, son," she said, turning up her wrinkled cheek for a kiss from Mr. Lake, then coming forward to greet the rest of the family.

Stevie gave her grandmother a critical look as the old woman hugged her daughter-in-law. In some ways Grandma Lake looked a lot like Stevie remembered her. She still had bright blue eyes and a thick mop of curly white hair cropped short around her ears. But had her face always been so deeply lined? Had the grid of wrinkles been as extensive? Had there been such large dark circles under her eyes before? Stevie struggled to recall earlier days, but it seemed so far in the past.

Grandma Lake turned and saw her. "Stevie!" she exclaimed. "Look at you. I think you've grown at least a foot since the last picture your father sent me." She stepped forward and took Stevie by the shoulders, kissing her soundly on both cheeks.

Stevie couldn't help feeling how her grandmother's hands trembled as they grasped her. And she couldn't help noticing how dry and paper-thin the skin of the elderly woman's cheeks felt as they brushed her own. "Hi, Grandma," she said. "I'm glad you came."

After all the greetings were over with, the family moved away from the gate, heading toward the long hallway leading to the lot where Mr. Lake had parked the car. Stevie noticed that her grandmother was walking quite slowly.

Mr. Lake noticed, too. "I have an idea," he said. "I'll run and fetch the car and meet the rest of you by that door right over there. No sense in all of us making that trek."

Grandma Lake nodded, once again looking grateful. "That would be wonderful, son," she said. "My flight was exhausting. I wouldn't mind sitting for a moment or two."

Mr. Lake handed his mother's suitcases to Chad, then hurried off. As Mrs. Lake helped Grandma Lake find a free bench near the door, Stevie glanced at her brothers. She could tell that they were all thinking the same thing she was. Since when had their cool, commanding, active grandmother become such a feeble old woman?

* * *

"I CAN'T BELIEVE she fell asleep in the car on the way home," Chad said. "Especially after not seeing any of us for so long. She never would have done that in the old days. She would have talked our ears off—*we* would have been the ones who got exhausted from answering all her questions. I guess that should tell us something about how the last five years have changed her."

Stevie leaned back on her pillow. She and her brothers were holding a furtive emergency meeting in her bedroom while their parents showed Grandma Lake to her room. "I guess she is getting old and frail now, like we were saying earlier," she said.

"That means we really should be careful while she's here," Alex said.

Chad furrowed his brow, looking worried. "You said it," he said. "I mean, I know we were sort of talking about that before. But this is really serious now."

For once, Stevie was in complete agreement with her brothers. "No kidding," she said. "Grandma probably can't deal with too much excitement. We'll have to make sure things stay calm around here while she's visiting."

"Okay," Michael said, nodding solemnly from his spot on the floor near Stevie's door. "What do we do?"

"First of all, we call a truce," Stevie said. "No matter what anyone in this room did to anyone else, or what anyone *thinks* anyone did to anyone else . . ." She paused, starting to feel a little confused by her own phrasing.

Chad stepped in and took over for her. "No fighting," he said briskly. "No insults, no matter how funny."

"Got it," Alex said. "So no matter how much Stevie stinks like a horse, we won't say a word. We won't even neigh and pretend it's a cough."

Stevie made a face at him. "And no matter how many zits Alex has on his nose, I won't make a single joke about Mount Vesuvius erupting on his face."

Chad frowned at them. "This is serious, you two," he said. "We don't want to make Grandma sick."

Stevie thought about that for a second. It would be terrible if their behavior endangered Grandma Lake's health. And she was only here for two weeks. The least her grandchildren could do was make her stay as pleasant and as soothing as possible. "You're right, Chad," she said. "We've got to be on our best behavior. All of us," she added, shooting a glance at Alex. "No pranks or practical jokes."

"No revenge plots," Chad said.

"No horsing around," Alex put in.

Stevie shot him another look, suspicious at his choice of words. But he spread his hands apologetically.

"Sorry," he said. "You know what I mean. We have to act civilized and stuff, like Mom and Dad were saying earlier."

"So for two weeks, all we have to do is act like good, quiet kids and not fight with each other, right?" Michael said.

Stevie nodded firmly. "It won't be easy," she said, "but we have no choice. Grandma's life may depend on it."

THE NEXT DAY was Saturday. Even though school was out for winter break, it was still The Saddle Club's favorite day of the week. That was because it was the day that their Pony Club, Horse Wise, met at Pine Hollow.

"Guess what," Carole said when she found Lisa in the tack room.

Lisa looked up from the saddle she was grabbing. "What?"

Carole grinned. "Britt is riding Coconut today. All I had to do was drop the teeniest hint to Max, and he jumped at the idea. I guess he thought that Britt and Coconut would get along just great."

Lisa couldn't help laughing at the smug look on her

friend's face. "Oh yeah?" she said. "Well, I'm sure she'll love him." She hoisted the saddle onto her shoulder. "But I'm also sure that she'll love Applesauce even—"

Lisa bit off the rest of the sentence just in time, as Britt appeared in the doorway of the tack room. Carole turned and saw her, too.

"Hi, Britt," Carole said with an innocent smile. "Can I help you find your tack? Which horse are you riding today?"

Lisa almost snorted, but she held it in. She didn't want to make Britt suspicious and spoil the surprise.

"Um, Max said I should try Coconut today," Britt replied.

The words were hardly out of her mouth when Carole had grabbed the correct saddle from its rack. She handed it to Britt, then pointed out Coconut's bridle. "Enjoy," she said cheerfully. "He's a terrific horse. I'm sure you'll get along famously."

"Speaking of terrific horses," Lisa said quickly, "I was just thinking about those Hedgerow horses. It was fun having them stay here last week, wasn't it? I kind of miss them now that they're gone."

Out of the corner of her eye, Lisa could see Carole rolling her eyes. But she ignored her. Britt was nodding. "They were nice horses," she said.

"Hey, I just had a great idea!" Lisa exclaimed. "Why don't we go visit them tomorrow? I'd love to see their new stable. What do you say?"

"Sorry," Carole said, not sounding sorry at all. "I can't make it. My dad and I are going to the movies."

Britt didn't answer one way or the other. She just stood quietly, carefully brushing little bits of dust off the saddle she was holding. Lisa realized that the shy girl probably didn't even understand that she was included in the invitation. *What would it be like to feel so insignificant?* Lisa wondered. *To just assume that people aren't talking to you—even when they are?* She decided it must be awfully lonely.

"So, how about it, Britt?" Lisa said. "Will you come with me tomorrow? It will be fun."

Britt looked up quickly. "Me?" she said. "You want me to come with you?"

"Sure," Lisa said. "What do you say? We can see how all our old friends are settling into their new home."

"Um, okay," Britt said. "I guess that would be okay."

"Great," Lisa said happily. She shot Carole a triumphant glance. "I'll get my mom to drive us over there. We'll have a great time."

A FEW MINUTES LATER Carole and Lisa had tacked up their horses for the meeting and were leading them toward the indoor ring. Carole held the bridle of her horse, a bay gelding named Starlight, as he danced sideways in anticipation of his morning's exercise. For once, Carole hardly noticed her horse's antics.

"Where could she be?" she said anxiously, glancing at her watch.

Lisa shook her head. She was leading a slender Thoroughbred mare named Prancer, the Pine Hollow horse she usually rode. "Late as usual, I guess," she said.

They were talking about Stevie, who had not yet appeared at the stable. That was bad news, since Max hated it when his students were late. Carole and Lisa were a little early for the meeting—none of the other students were in the ring yet. But even if Stevie arrived at Pine Hollow immediately, she would have to rush to get her horse and herself ready in time.

"We'd better tack up Belle for her," Carole said. She looked around and spotted Polly Giacomin coming into the ring, leading her own horse, Romeo. "Hi, Polly," Carole called. "Can you do us a favor?"

"Sure," Polly said. "What is it?" Once the other two girls had explained their problem, Polly agreed to keep an eye on their horses.

Carole and Lisa hurried out of the indoor ring and down the aisle toward the tack room. They grabbed Belle's tack and headed for the mare's stall. On the way, Carole noticed Magoo poking his head out over the half door of his stall.

"Hold on," she said. "Let's just give him a quick look." She slung Belle's bridle over her shoulder and then swung open Magoo's stall door.

Lisa peered over Carole's shoulder. "Oh no," she said in dismay. "I guess he likes hot sauce!"

The gelding had ripped off the bandages the girls had

treated with the spicy sauce. What's more, he had managed to remove a few more that they hadn't thought he would be able to reach.

"He must have been really determined to get those off," Carole said, leaning closer to examine a wound on Magoo's shoulder. The bandage was hanging by one side, and Carole guessed that the horse had rubbed against the wall of his stall to make it come loose.

Lisa bent to retrieve a bandage that was lying near the front of the stall. She turned it over in her hand. "It looks like he just nibbled around the parts with the hot sauce," she said. "Mrs. Reg won't believe it. She swore it was a foolproof plan."

"We'll have to deal with this after Horse Wise," Carole said with a sigh. "He must have been lying down after he took the bandages off—there's all kinds of straw and dirt in these wounds. What a mess."

Lisa shook her head and patted Magoo on the nose as Carole latched the door shut behind them. "You're not an easy patient, Magoo," she said. "Anyone would think you didn't *want* us to help you. Don't you want to get better so you can go back home and see all your friends at Hedgerow?"

"Come on," Carole said. "We'd better get going or Belle will never be ready in time."

A few minutes later, Lisa was just getting ready to fasten the noseband on Belle's bridle when Stevie appeared outside the stall, red-faced and panting.

"Whew!" she exclaimed, clutching her side. "I didn't think I was going to make it. I . . ."

She paused for breath, her chest heaving. Lisa finished fastening the noseband and then handed the reins to Stevie. "Don't worry," she said. "You're all ready to go."

Carole nodded. "Now let's get over to the ring before we're all late."

Stevie followed her friends down the aisle with Belle in tow. She mopped her brow with one sleeve and shook her head. "You'll never believe why I was late," she said once she had caught her breath. "My idiot twin brother hid my riding boots."

"So what else is new?" Carole said. "Usually you just throttle him until he tells you where he put them."

"I couldn't do that today," Stevie said. "That's the problem." She quickly filled her friends in on the situation with her grandmother. "So we made a pact. We're all going to be on our best behavior for two whole weeks," she finished.

Lisa grinned. "It sounds like Alex didn't get the message. Otherwise he wouldn't have hidden your boots."

"Well, no," Stevie admitted grudgingly. "He hid them before we made the pact." She paused. "At least that's what he claims. He says he just forgot to tell me about it until he noticed me tiptoeing around this morning peeking in closets and stuff."

Carole giggled at the thought of Stevie tiptoeing around and peeking daintily into closets in search of her boots. Stevie's usual method of searching was to stampede around, yelling and throwing things, until she found whatever she was looking for. And, Carole had to admit, that usually seemed to be the most effective method of finding things in the chaotic Lake household.

Lisa was thinking the same thing. "So you four are really going to be good while your grandmother is here?" she asked. "I'll believe that when I see it!"

Stevie looked a little hurt. "I mean it," she said. "And so do my brothers. We want to make sure Grandma doesn't get too stressed out while she's here. And for someone in her condition, just hanging around my house the way it usually is could be pretty stressful."

"I guess that might be true," Carole said. "So where were your boots, anyway?"

Stevie stopped walking and held up one foot. Her boot was coated with a fine gray dust. "He stuffed them up the fireplace flue." She slapped one ankle against the other, and a cloud of ash flew upward. Even Belle wrinkled her nose.

"Yuck," Lisa said as they all resumed walking. They were almost at the indoor ring by now. "It's a good thing nobody decided to light a fire."

"A good thing for Alex," Stevie agreed as she led Belle into the ring and toward her friends' horses. "But he's still going to be sorry he pulled this."

Lisa raised an eyebrow. "Wait a minute," she said. "Didn't you just finish telling us you're not going to pull any pranks or exact any elaborate forms of revenge while your grandmother is staying with you?"

"Exactly," Stevie said. She grinned wickedly. "That means I have two whole weeks to plan what I'm going to do to him after she leaves."

MAX SPENT MOST of the Horse Wise meeting talking about the gymkhana and having the students practice some of the skills they would need for it. Normally every second Horse Wise meeting was an unmounted one, when the students learned about non-riding aspects of horse care and stable management. But Max was making an exception to that schedule for the gymkhana, which would take place in exactly one week.

"After all," he said with a grin before dismissing the students, "I guess you ought to have some fun next weekend, since school starts again the following Monday."

A groan went up from the riders. Then they all dismounted and led their horses toward the door.

"By the way," Stevie told her friends as they walked out together, "I don't think I ever thanked you guys for tacking up Belle for me. You really saved my neck this time. I owe you one."

"Oh yeah?" Carole said with a grin. She winked at Lisa. "If you really mean that, I can think of one way you could pay us back. You could take care of Magoo all by yourself today."

Stevie gave a mock groan. But then she grinned.

"You've got it," she said cheerfully. "It's the least I can do. If it weren't for you guys, I'd be in even worse shape than he is—once Max got through with me, that is."

HALF AN HOUR later, Magoo was already looking much more presentable. Stevie had cleaned the hay and dirt off him and replaced all the missing bandages. This time she decided to be more liberal with the hot sauce. She was careful once again to avoid getting it on his skin, but she made sure that if the horse nibbled on *these* bandages he would definitely taste them.

"There," she told the horse as she applied a few more drops to a bandage near the crest of his neck. "I know there's no way you could reach this one with your teeth, but better safe than sorry, right?"

"Hi, Stevie," said a quiet voice from outside the stall. "How's Magoo?"

Stevie glanced up. "Hi, Britt," she said. "He's ornery, as usual. But he's doing okay. How's it going?"

"Okay," Britt replied. Then she fell silent. She leaned on the half door of the stall and watched as Stevie screwed the cap back onto the hot sauce bottle.

Once the bottle was back in the grooming bucket, Stevie looked up at the other girl again. Britt smiled shyly, but she still didn't say anything more. Stevie guessed that the new girl was trying to be friendly but wasn't quite sure how to go about it.

She decided to help her out. "Horse Wise was fun today, wasn't it?" she said cheerfully. "I can't wait for the gymkhana."

Britt nodded. "It sounds like fun," she agreed. "Gymkhanas were one of my favorite things at my old stable. We always had really silly games and things."

Stevie was pretty sure that that was the longest she had ever heard Britt speak at one time. That was a good sign. Maybe the shy girl was starting to open up at last. "They're one of my favorite things, too," Stevie said, grabbing a comb and starting to work a tangle out of Magoo's mane while she talked. "And I bet that snowball race will be a blast. I'm going to tell Max about it the first chance I get. I'll make sure he knows the snowball part was your idea."

Britt's cheeks turned slightly pink. "Oh, that's okay," she said modestly. "The race was mostly your idea. You probably would have thought of the snowballs yourself sooner or later."

Stevie hardly heard the other girl's comment. That was because she had just peeked into Magoo's manger. "Oh, it figures," she said.

"What's wrong?" Britt asked.

Stevie grabbed a handful of alfalfa pellets out of the manger and held them out for Britt to see. "He ate everything else and left these," she said. "It's the first time he's done that."

"Do you think there's something wrong with him?" Britt asked, looking concerned.

Stevie shrugged. "I'll mention it to Max so he can tell Judy when she stops by," she said. "But my guess is that Magoo just decided he didn't like alfalfa pellets anymore. Or else he got bored and decided it would be fun to eat around them this time." She gave the horse an annoyed look. "It just figures you would be a picky eater too, Magoo."

Britt giggled uncertainly, seeming unsure whether Stevie was joking or not. "Maybe to him, alfalfa pellets taste like broccoli does to me," she said.

It took Stevie a second to realize that Britt had actually made a joke. Then she grinned in appreciation. "Good one," she said. "You're thinking like a horse. Carole would definitely approve." Stevie herself was starting to approve of Britt. The new girl was smart and funny underneath that shy exterior, though it took her a while to show it. But she *did* seem to be making more of an effort lately.

Just then, Polly walked by. She paused beside Britt to glance in at Magoo. "How's the patient?" she asked Stevie.

"Oh, he's all right," Stevie said. "Have you met Britt?" She quickly introduced the two girls.

Polly gave the new girl a friendly nod. "I've seen you around," she said. "How do you like Pine Hollow so far?"

"I like it fine," Britt said softly. "You're the one who rides that pretty brown gelding, right?"

Suddenly Stevie remembered something. When Britt

had toured Pine Hollow on her first visit, she had seen Polly's horse, Romeo, in his stall and mentioned that he resembled her own horse back in Ohio. "That's right," she said. "Polly just got him recently. His name is Romeo."

"He looks like a really nice horse," Britt said.

"Thanks," Polly said, looking pleased. "He is pretty terrific." She turned to Stevie. "That reminds me," she said. "Romeo's breeder called me last night. He's got another horse for sale—Romeo's half brother, actually. I promised to spread the word around here. Do you know anyone who's looking?"

"Hmm," Stevie said, pretending to think about Polly's question. Meanwhile, her mind was racing. This could be the answer! It seemed almost too perfect. Romeo was a friendly, cheerful, talented, and eager-to-please young horse. If his half brother was anything like him, he would be absolutely perfect for Britt. He would have enough spunk to challenge her riding abilities, but no major character or behavior problems to overwhelm her own timid personality. Stevie had to fight to keep from showing how excited she was at this unexpected piece of luck. "I'll have to think about it, Polly," she said.

"Okay," Polly said. "Let me know." She said good-bye and headed down the aisle.

Stevie waited a minute or two. She didn't want Britt to get suspicious, but she had to talk to Polly. Keeping her face neutral, she started to roll a bandage around Magoo's injured hock. Then she looked up at Britt, who was watching silently.

"You know," Stevie said, creasing her brow a little. "I wonder if I should tell Max about Magoo's feed problem now instead of later. He might want to call Judy right away."

Britt shrugged. "Like you said, it's probably nothing serious, right?" she said.

"Probably," Stevie agreed truthfully. "Just the same, I think I'll go catch him before he disappears somewhere or other. Do you know how to wrap a hock?"

Britt nodded. "Sure," she said. "I'll finish that if you want."

"Thanks." Stevie held the stall door for her as she came inside. Then she quickly let herself out and hurried down the aisle. She didn't break into a grin until she was absolutely sure that Britt wouldn't see her.

"COULD YOU PLEASE pass the butter, Chad?" Stevie asked in a low, discreet tone.

Chad picked up the butter dish, which was sitting near his place at the dinner table. "Certainly, Stevie," he replied calmly. "Here you go."

Stevie accepted the butter dish with a smile. "Thank you so much, Chad," she said. "I really appreciate it." She carefully put a small pat of butter on her plate, then turned to her twin. "Would you like any butter, Alex?"

"No thank you, Stevie," Alex replied. He dabbed at his mouth with his napkin, then returned it carefully to his lap. "But it was nice of you to ask."

Stevie thought she caught her parents exchanging perplexed glances. She smiled secretly. So far the plan seemed to be working perfectly. That afternoon, after returning home from Pine Hollow, Stevie had volunteered to help her mother make dinner while her father talked to Grandma Lake in the living room. Mrs. Lake had seemed surprised at the offer, to say the least, but she hadn't said anything about it.

Neither she nor Mr. Lake had made any comment about their children's behavior at the dinner table, either. Not even when Alex had complimented Michael on his T-shirt, or when Stevie had asked Chad how he had enjoyed his basketball practice that day.

But they looked more amazed than ever a few minutes later, when Chad turned to Stevie with a courteous smile. "So, Stevie," he said, "how was Pine Hollow today?"

At that, Alex couldn't suppress a groan. "Do we really have to know?" he complained.

Stevie shot him a quick, murderous glance. Then she smiled sweetly at Chad. "Actually, Chad," she said, "there's not much to tell." That wasn't true, of course. There was lots to talk about—Magoo's progress, next weekend's gymkhana, her talks with Britt and Polly, and all the usual interesting stuff that went on at the stable all the time. But Stevie was afraid that any of those topics might stir up too much excitement for her grandmother. "Why don't we talk about—um—Mom's plans for her garden this summer?" *There*, she thought with satisfaction. *That should be a safe topic. Nice and dull.*

She sneaked a peek at her grandmother's face. Grandma Lake looked a bit startled. *Uh-oh*, Stevie thought. *I guess Alex's obnoxious comment upset her even more than I thought.*

She scanned her mind for a way to take the old woman's mind off her brother's behavior. Suddenly inspiration struck. "I have a great idea," she chirped. "Why don't we go to the Smithsonian while you're here, Grandma?" The world-famous Smithsonian Institution was only a short drive away in Washington, D.C. It consisted of all sorts of museums, from modern art to natural history to aviation. Stevie was sure that that would be a nice, soothing way for her grandmother to spend the day, as long as they didn't do too much fast walking. And older people always liked to do cultural stuff, right?

Sure enough, Grandma Lake was nodding. "That sounds like fun," she said. "Which museums do you want to see? How about the National Air and Space Museum? Is that one still your favorite?"

It was, but Stevie quickly shook her head. The Air and Space Museum! That had to be the most exciting one of all. Stevie shuddered at the thought of what stimulating stories of space travel and thrilling tales of early flight might do to her grandmother's heart rate. *Grandma Lake probably thinks a young whippersnapper like me can only appreciate an exciting museum like that*, Stevie thought. *But something quieter would be much better.*

She tried to think of the quietest, most boring museum

of the bunch. "Actually," she said, stirring her peas with her fork, "I've been wanting to visit the National Gallery of Art. Could we go there instead?"

Grandma Lake looked surprised, but she nodded. "Sure, Stevie. If that's where you really want to go."

"Oh, I do," Stevie assured her. "I really do." *There*, she thought with relief. *A bunch of pictures should be just the thing. Grandma will love it.*

Stevie's mother was staring at her suspiciously. She had dragged Stevie through the National Gallery of Art a couple of years ago, and Stevie had complained the entire time about how dull it was. But Mrs. Lake didn't comment on her daughter's sudden interest in art. "That sounds like a nice plan," she said, passing Grandma Lake the bowl of peas. "We can all go on Monday if you like."

Grandma Lake took the bowl and helped herself to a second serving. "So, Stevie," she said, "your parents tell me you've been spending more time than ever at that stable of yours lately. But you've hardly said a word about it. I want to hear all about it."

Stevie gulped. How could she possibly make Pine Hollow sound unexciting? "Like I said before, there's not much to tell," she said. "Not much happens there. You know, we ride, we take lessons—pretty boring, really."

There was a small, strangled sound from Alex at that, but Stevie was pretty sure her grandmother hadn't heard it. After all, didn't they say that your hearing was the first thing to go?

"You're being unusually subdued on this topic, Stevie," her father said. "Did something happen at the stable today to upset you? You didn't get into a fight with your friends, did you?"

"Oh, no, no," Stevie said quickly. "It was just an average day." She couldn't believe her father's comment. Didn't he understand that she was only trying to save his own mother from unnecessary stress? "Um, we had a Horse Wise meeting today—that's our Pony Club," she told her grandmother. "Today we just rode in the indoor ring and practiced a few different things. It wasn't very interesting."

"Oh, but it must be so much fun to ride every day," Grandma Lake said. "And having your very own horse must be so exciting!"

"Not really," Stevie said, trying to sound sincere. "When you get right down to it, it's not much different than having a cat. Or, um, a goldfish or something."

Grandma Lake looked skeptical, but Stevie just smiled at her serenely. All three of Stevie's brothers were steadily shoveling food into their mouths. Stevie guessed that they were trying to keep themselves busy so that they wouldn't be tempted to make any jokes at her expense—or Pine Hollow's.

"Well, I think it would be more interesting than that," Grandma Lake said after a brief silence. "I hope I'll get a chance to meet your horse while I'm here, Stevie."

"I'm sure that can be arranged," Mrs. Lake said. "Stevie

loves showing people around Pine Hollow. Don't you, Stevie?"

"Oh, no. I've outgrown that, Mom," Stevie said earnestly. "I realized how dull it must be for people. Grandma would be bored silly."

Grandma Lake shook her head. "No, I wouldn't," she assured Stevie. "I'd love a tour. Which day is good for you?"

"You have a riding lesson on Tuesday, don't you, Stevie?" Mr. Lake said, looking up from his food. "How about if we bring your grandmother by then?"

"That sounds wonderful!" Grandma Lake exclaimed before Stevie could protest. "Tuesday it is."

"Um, are you sure?" Stevie asked. "I mean, it will probably be pretty boring. I think Max is going to spend the first half of the lesson just talking to us about bits or something dull like that."

Her mother and father exchanged glances. Stevie could tell that they were on the verge of demanding to know what was going on, but she guessed they didn't want to make a scene in front of Grandma Lake. For obvious reasons.

"All right, Stevie," Mrs. Lake said evenly. "If the first half of the lesson is going to be so dull, we'll show up for the second half. Maybe we can all go out for an early dinner in town afterward."

"That sounds perfect," Grandma Lake agreed, and Mr. Lake nodded.

Stevie smiled weakly as her grandmother turned to beam at her. How was she going to find a way around this?

THE NEXT DAY, Mrs. Atwood dropped Lisa and Britt off at Hedgerow Farms' main gate. "Have a nice time, girls," Mrs. Atwood said. "I'll be back to pick you up after I finish my shopping."

"Thanks, Mom," Lisa said. "Come on, Britt. Let's go."

Lisa smiled with anticipation. Now that Britt was here, she was sure to fall in love with Applesauce just as Lisa had imagined. Stevie had called the night before to tell her about Romeo's half brother, but she wasn't worried about that, or about Coconut, either. Applesauce was the one for Britt. Lisa just knew it.

The two girls walked up the gracefully curving driveway toward the brand-new stable building. The air was crisp but not too cold, and only a few clouds drifted across the grayish blue winter sky.

"It's a nice day," Britt offered timidly.

"It sure is," Lisa said. "Especially for January." Normally she wouldn't be excited to be talking about the weather, but the fact that Britt was making conversation at all was a big step for her. Lisa wanted to encourage that.

When they reached the stable yard, they found Elaine, Hedgerow's manager, watching as one of her stable hands longed a horse in a small paddock. Elaine had broken her leg before Christmas, and it was still in a cast. Lisa and Britt joined the woman by the paddock fence.

"Hi there, girls," Elaine said, leaning on her crutches. Lisa had called the day before to tell her they were coming. Elaine turned to Britt with a friendly smile. "You must be the new girl I've heard so much about."

Britt blushed. "I'm Britt," she said softly. "Nice to meet you."

Elaine nodded good-naturedly, then turned to Lisa. "So how's Magoo doing? Judy calls every day or two to give me an update, but I haven't heard from her today."

"He's fine," Lisa said. "More or less, anyway." She and Carole had met at Pine Hollow that morning to deal with their patient. He had given up on the bandages after Stevie's latest hot-sauce application, but he had managed to get a large piece of straw into his eye, which was red and watery when the girls had arrived. They were pretty sure they had caught it before it turned into full-fledged conjunctivitis, but they had called Judy to let her know what had happened, just in case.

Lisa filled Elaine in on the whole story. The woman shook her head ruefully. "That Magoo," she said with a little laugh. "He really is an equine hypochondriac, isn't he? He loves to be fussed over. I just hope he recovers pretty soon. I was trying to sell him before the accident, and I've already had a couple of calls from potential buyers who want to check him out when he's better."

Lisa nodded politely. She hoped Magoo got better soon, too—mostly because he was so much extra work for The Saddle Club. But right now she was more interested in Britt. They didn't have much time before Mrs. Atwood returned, and Lisa wanted to make sure that Britt had plenty of time to get to know Applesauce.

"Do you mind if we go inside and say hello?" she said. "We miss all your horses already. Right, Britt?"

Britt nodded and followed Lisa obediently into the stable building.

Lisa didn't want to be too obvious about her intentions, so she and Britt stopped at a few stalls before they reached Applesauce's. Britt seemed honestly delighted to see each and every horse again, though her only comment was invariably "What a nice horse."

Lisa was sure she would have more to say about Applesauce. But when the Appaloosa nuzzled Britt's palm looking for treats, Britt just smiled. "What a nice horse," she said, patting Applesauce on the neck.

"She really is nice, isn't she?" Lisa said encouragingly. "I think she might be my favorite of all the Hedgerow horses. She's so calm, and sweet, and smart, and nice . . ."

Britt nodded agreeably, but she didn't say anything.

"What about you, Britt?" Lisa prompted. "If you had to pick your favorite horse in this entire stable, which would it be?" She realized she wasn't being exactly subtle, but she couldn't help it. Britt just wasn't responding the way she was supposed to.

"Oh, I don't know," Britt said. She paused and ran her fingers through Applesauce's mane. "I love all of them equally, I guess." She gave Applesauce a final pat, then moved on to the next stall.

Lisa sighed and followed. She was disappointed that her plan wasn't working so far. But she had to admit one thing: Britt seemed just as horse-crazy as the members of The Saddle Club. She obviously adored every horse she met, and they all adored her right back. It was as true here as it was at Pine Hollow.

It's just too bad she's so shy that she hasn't made many human *friends yet,* Lisa thought.

Suddenly she stopped in the middle of the aisle. Britt was already greeting the next horse, so she didn't notice. Lisa's face slowly spread into a wide grin. She had just had an idea for another very interesting Saddle Club project. . . .

"STEVIE?" LISA SAID a few hours later, pressing the phone to her ear. She was still excited about her idea. Her friends had both been out all day—Stevie with her grandmother and Carole with her father. But Stevie had finally picked up the phone.

"Oh, hi, Lisa," Stevie said, sounding distracted. "Listen, I can't really talk right now. Grandma is alone with

Michael, and I'm afraid he'll forget our plan and start showing her his superhero comic book collection or something. Besides, I promised I'd let her teach me to play bridge."

Lisa groaned. "Ugh. How boring." Her parents had taught her the card game already, and she hated it. She couldn't imagine Stevie sitting down to a bridge game. "But hold on just a second, okay? I promise I'll make this quick. I want to tell you and Carole at the same time. It's important."

Stevie hesitated for a second, then agreed. "Hold on," she said. "I'll get her." Stevie's phone was the only one with three-way calling.

Lisa waited while Stevie put her on hold to dial Carole's number. A moment later all three girls were on the line together. "What's your big news, Lisa?" Carole asked. "Don't tell me Britt actually chose Applesauce!"

"No way," Stevie protested. "She can't! She hasn't even met Romeo's brother yet."

"No, no," Lisa said hastily. "That's not what my news is about—although it does have something to do with Britt. It's an idea for a new Saddle Club project."

"What is it?" Carole asked expectantly.

Lisa took a deep breath. She had no idea how her friends would react to her idea. But there was only one way to find out.

"What would you think," she said, "of considering Britt for membership in The Saddle Club?"

54

"HOW DOES HE do it?" Lisa asked, exasperated. "How does he manage to have some new problem every single day?"

She and Carole were in Magoo's stall. It was Monday, so the two girls were on their own while Stevie visited the Smithsonian with her family. Today Magoo's bandages were still intact. He had eaten all of his food. And his eye seemed to be all right. But he had been coughing since the girls had arrived that day, and Red O'Malley, the head stable hand, had stopped by to tell them that Magoo had been coughing frequently since the night before.

Carole sighed. "I guess he caught a cold," she said. Even though she was sure that Red had already done so, she felt the gelding's esophagus area carefully to make sure that a food blockage wasn't causing the cough. But from the look of the horse, Carole was pretty sure that the cause was a mild upper-respiratory infection. "Red said Judy promised to stop by and check on him to make sure that's all it is."

"Did I hear someone mention my name?" Judy asked cheerfully from outside the stall.

Carole and Lisa greeted the vet and stepped aside to give her room. Judy quickly checked over Magoo's injuries, complimenting the girls on their nursing.

"We won't lie to you," Lisa said. "It hasn't been easy. Elaine called him an equine hypochondriac, and I think she's right."

Judy laughed heartily at that. She continued her examination, then finally stepped back and reached for her battered vet bag, which she had left in the aisle. "He's got a slight cold," she said. "I don't think it's too serious." She dug through the bag and came up with a container of medicine, which she handed to Carole. "Just keep him warm and put this into a hot bran mash for him. The dosage is on the label. He should be fine in a day or two."

Carole took the medicine. "Okay," she said, "but I'm sure he'll have managed to come down with something else by then."

Judy laughed again and gave Magoo a pat on the neck. "Don't listen to her, boy," she said. "I know you can't help it, you fussy thing."

"We know that, too," Carole said, immediately feeling

bad about her comment. She knew that Magoo hadn't gotten sick on purpose. It just *seemed* like he had. "We're a little frustrated, that's all."

"I know," Judy said. "But you're doing a good job. Magoo is getting better under your care—slowly, but he is getting better. Just keep at it."

Carole and Lisa nodded. Judy packed up her bag and left with a wave.

When the girls were once again alone with the horse, Lisa sighed. "I feel kind of bad about complaining, too," she said. "I mean, usually I like fussing over a horse as much as anybody. Magoo is just so hard to figure out sometimes, you know?"

"I know," Carole said. She glanced down at the container of medicine she was still holding. "Come on, I guess we'd better get started on that mash."

Lisa picked up Magoo's feed bucket. Just as they headed out for the grain shed, Britt came toward them, smiling tentatively.

"Hi," she said. "I just stopped by to see how you're doing with Magoo."

Carole and Lisa exchanged secret smiles. Carole had been thinking about Lisa's idea ever since The Saddle Club's phone conversation the night before. She was starting to think it was a really good one. Britt *did* seem to be making an effort to be friendly toward The Saddle Club.

Carole smiled at the new girl, trying to imagine how it

would be to have her join their little group. The Saddle Club had a number of out-of-town members, but that wasn't the same thing. If Britt joined, she would be a full-time member, just like Carole, Lisa, and Stevie. What would that be like?

While Carole was thinking about that, Lisa was telling Britt about Magoo's latest ailment. When she was finished, Britt shyly offered to help make the bran mash Judy had prescribed.

"Sure," Carole said immediately. "We were just going to get started on it. Come on. We'd love some help."

Out of the corner of her eye, Carole saw Lisa winking at her. She guessed what her friend was thinking, because Carole was thinking the exact same thing. Not only was Britt horse-crazy, but here she was, offering to help out, just as though she were already a member of The Saddle Club!

The three girls headed for the grain shed first, where they measured out the correct amounts of bran and sweet feed into Magoo's bucket, adding some salt to the mix as well. Then they carried the bucket to the deep, wide sink in one corner of the tack room.

"Max had this installed recently," Carole explained to Britt, pointing to a small faucet set off to the side of the sink. "It provides instant boiling water, see?" She put the bucket under the faucet and turned it on, letting steamy water splash onto the grains. "It's really useful for making mashes and hot poultices and stuff like that."

Britt smiled. "I know," she said. "You told me that on the tour you gave me on my first day here. Several times, actually."

Lisa wasn't sure, but it sounded as though Britt was teasing Carole! That was a really good sign. If she was comfortable enough to start joking around with them, that meant she was already much more comfortable with them than she had been at first.

They covered the mash and carried it back to Magoo's stall. Setting it aside to cool, they went to work replacing his bandages and making sure his wounds were clean and healing properly. Britt pitched in willingly, even offering to redo the bandage on his hock, which was the trickiest one to do.

While they worked, the girls talked. They decided to try brainstorming more ideas for the gymkhana, since they still hadn't come up with anything except the snow-ball race. They missed Stevie's input, but even without her they managed to come up with some good ideas to suggest to Max. Britt didn't contribute as much to the conversation as either of the others, but she contributed some. Both Carole and Lisa thought that was a good start for their potential new best friend.

They were debating the merits of a blindfolded relay race when they finished working on Magoo.

"That should do it," Carole said as she smoothed down the last bandage. "We should probably give him his bran mash and then leave him to eat in peace."

Lisa watched as Carole carefully measured the proper dosage of medicine into the lukewarm mash. "What do you say we move this little meeting into the locker room?" she suggested.

Britt bit her lip. "Um . . . ," she began.

"What is it, Britt?" Carole asked, hanging the bucket in the stall. Magoo stuck his nose into it eagerly as soon as she moved out of the way.

Britt shrugged. "Well, it's just that I saw that girl Veronica in the locker room before I came over here," she said. "And, well, you know . . ."

"Enough said." Lisa winked. "Don't worry, Britt. We don't like to hang out with Veronica any more than you do."

Britt looked relieved. "Good," she said. "Then maybe we should just stay here with Magoo. He doesn't seem to mind."

Sure enough, the horse hardly noticed their presence as he slurped down the tasty mash. Because of his general fussiness, Carole had been worried that Magoo would refuse to eat the mash if he sensed a foreign taste. Fortunately, he didn't seem to notice the taste of the medicine.

"All right," Carole said. "We'll stay here."

"Good," Britt said quickly. She glanced down at the grooming bucket at her feet. "Maybe when he's done eating, Magoo would like a little extra grooming or something."

Lisa nodded. She was pretty sure that Britt was just

coming up with an excuse to keep them in the stall—and out of Veronica's path—for as long as possible. That was fine with her. The last thing she felt like doing was spending even more time fussing over Magoo, and she was sure Carole would agree. But it would be worth it if it helped them get to know Britt better.

Carole was thinking the same thing. She leaned against the wall and watched the horse eat. "At this rate we should be able to come up with some great ideas for the gymkhana," she said. "Stevie will be awfully jealous when she learns we left her out, though."

Lisa giggled. "Don't worry about her," she said. "That's what she gets for going off to have fun at the Smithsonian and leaving us here with all the work."

STEVIE WASN'T HAVING much fun at that moment. She was stifling a yawn as her mother, father, and grandmother oohed and aahed over yet another boring, stuffy old oil painting.

The worst part was, her brothers weren't even there suffering with her. They had all managed to come up with excuses not to join today's trip. Chad had claimed to have an extra basketball practice. Alex wanted to catch up on his homework before school started again. And Michael had been invited to a friend's house for the afternoon.

But the museum trip had been Stevie's idea, so she was stuck. How long had she been in this dull place, anyway? It felt like hours. She hadn't realized quite how big the

National Gallery was, or she would have suggested some-place smaller—like the Willow Creek Art Museum, for instance. That only had three rooms.

"Coming, Stevie?" her father asked as he and the other adults moved on to another painting.

Stevie shuffled along behind him. She had nothing against art. But why were art museums always so dry and stuffy and dull?

She stole a glance at her grandmother. Grandma Lake was gazing at the next picture, a dark oil portrait of a pudgy woman in old-fashioned dress. An ugly little pooch was perched on her ample lap. Both dog and woman looked grumpy and uncomfortable. Stevie knew exactly how they felt.

As Stevie watched, her grandmother raised her hand to her mouth to cover a yawn. Stevie frowned. They had done a lot of walking already today. She hoped her grand-mother wasn't getting too exhausted by all the exercise.

"I'm kind of tired," Stevie said as her parents got ready to move on to another painting. "Do you mind if we sit down for a few minutes?" She gestured to an empty bench in the center of the room.

Mr. Lake shrugged. "I suppose so," he said. "Although I don't understand how you could be tired already, Stevie. We've only been here for half an hour. What happened to all that youthful energy you usually have?"

Grandma Lake laughed as Stevie led the way to the bench. "I understand," she told her son. "You were the same way as a boy. Art museums are the only place in the world that are more tiring when you're young than when you're old." She winked at Stevie. "Except maybe for department stores."

Stevie smiled as Grandma Lake sat down beside her. She didn't care how much the adults made fun of her. The important thing was making sure her grandmother got a chance to rest.

As the others chatted about the paintings in the room, Stevie let her mind drift to more interesting things. She wondered if her friends had finished taking care of Magoo yet. She also wondered if they had made any progress on either of their current Saddle Club projects. Since Stevie couldn't do much to help with those while she was stuck here, she decided to try to think up new ideas for the gymkhana. It was only a few days away, and she couldn't wait. That reminded her—The Saddle Club had already decided to ask Britt to be the fourth member of their gymkhana team, but they hadn't actually asked her yet. Stevie made a mental note to do it the next day at lessons.

Thinking about the next day's riding lesson reminded Stevie that her grandmother would be coming to watch. She sighed. She still had no idea what she was going to do to keep the old woman from becoming overly excited by all the action at the stable. There had to be a solution.

At least Grandma doesn't know about the gymkhana, Stevie reminded herself thankfully. She could hardly imagine what might happen if her grandmother came to watch something *that* action-packed and exciting! She would probably have a stroke on the spot.

A few minutes later, just as Grandma Lake covered another yawn, Mr. Lake stood up. "Ready to move on?" he asked Stevie.

Stevie gave her grandmother an anxious look. She was obviously still tired. But she stood up, and Stevie reluctantly did the same. Maybe she could try to walk really slowly so that everybody else would have to, too. That might help her grandmother.

Of course, it also means it will take us that much longer to get through this stupid museum, Stevie reminded herself grimly. Still, she didn't have much choice, did she? She would have to make the sacrifice for the sake of her grandmother's health.

The family moved into the next room and stopped in front of the first painting. This one showed a man with a droopy mustache holding up a sword.

Stevie stared at it. It looked almost identical to half a dozen of the pictures in the room they had just left. But her parents and grandmother gazed at it as if they had never seen a painting before in their lives. *I'm glad Grandma is enjoying herself,* Stevie thought glumly. *But if this is the kind of stuff I'll have to do with my time when I'm her age, then I never want to get old!*

6

"PLEASE, MAX?" STEVIE whined. "Pretty please with sugar on top? *Pleeeeeeeease?*"

Max crossed his arms over his chest and stared at her. "Let me get this straight," he said, leaning back against the desk in Mrs. Reg's office, where Stevie had cornered him. "You want me to spend the second half of today's class practicing *walking* skills? Is this really Stevie Lake standing before me?"

Stevie shrugged and grinned weakly. She knew that she was normally the last person in the world who would want to spend so much time doing something as dull as walking. But she was sure it was the best way to keep her grandmother from getting overexcited while watching their class. "Walking is an important gait," she reminded Max. "Isn't that what you're always telling us?"

Max just snorted. "I was planning to spend today polishing up your skills for the gymkhana," he said. "Some of the games will involve some complicated moves."

"I know," Stevie said. "We can practice those all you want before my grandma gets here. She's only coming for the second half of class."

Max still looked skeptical. "I don't really understand what you're so worried about, Stevie," he said. "I'm sure your grandmother can handle a normal lesson, or she wouldn't come. Besides, she's just watching, not riding." He grinned. "Although if she's related to you, I wouldn't be surprised if she ended up wanting to climb into the saddle and go for a brisk canter herself."

Stevie knew Max was only joking, but even the thought of her grandmother on horseback made her shudder. No, her plan was the best way. Max just didn't understand the seriousness of the situation.

She decided to take another tack. "Okay, I didn't want to resort to this," she said, narrowing her eyes a little. "But you leave me no choice." She paused for dramatic effect.

Max glanced at his watch. "Shouldn't you be tacking up Belle right now?" he said. "You don't want to be late for class."

"As I was saying," Stevie said, ignoring the interrup-

66

tion, "you leave me no choice. If you don't agree to stick to walking after my grandma gets here, I'll be forced to withhold all of my great new ideas for the gymkhana. You'll be stuck with nothing but lame stuff like Veronica's shopping spree race."

Max rolled his eyes. "Is that supposed to be a threat?" he said, not sounding very threatened. He glanced at his watch again. "Okay, fine. You win. Let me know when your family gets here, and we'll start walking."

"Really?" Stevie could hardly believe the ploy had worked. Actually, when she thought about it for a second, she suspected that Max was probably just tired of listening to her arguments and wanted to shut her up. But she didn't care. She was getting her way, and that was all that mattered.

HALF AN HOUR into the lesson, Stevie was busy guiding Belle through a figure eight at a brisk trot. The mare responded beautifully to every command, and when they finished the figure, Stevie gave her a proud pat on the neck.

Then she glanced over at the doorway to the indoor ring, as she had been doing frequently throughout the lesson. She was just in time to see her entire family enter, with her grandmother leading the way.

"Um, Max?" she called, waving her hand at the instructor, who was mounted in the center of the ring. "Would you mind if I said hello to my *grandmother*?" She carefully stressed the last word, hoping that Max would remember his promise.

Max looked from Stevie to Grandma Lake, then back again. He sighed. "Sure, Stevie," he said. "Be my guest." He raised his voice for the whole class to hear. "Okay, everybody. For the rest of our time today we're going to get some practice at the walk. Please take your horses around the ring counterclockwise at a slow, steady gait. I want to see perfect form out there, people."

Stevie waved at her family, ignoring the whispers and murmurs that were rising around her. Max often asked them to walk as part of their classes. As he liked to point out, it was helpful to practice even the most basic of skills on a regular basis. But the students were understandably surprised that he wanted them to spend so much time walking just four days before the gymkhana.

"Did he say to walk?" Stevie overheard Polly Giacomin ask Lorraine Olsen. "But I didn't get to do the figure eight yet!"

Veronica diAngelo was more direct. "Max!" she called out loudly. "What are you talking about? Do you really want us to just walk around the ring? Why?"

Max gave her a stern look. "Who's the instructor around here, me or you?" he barked.

Stevie grinned at the sullen look on Veronica's face. Even obnoxious Veronica was afraid to talk back to Max when he used that tone. She just shrugged and yanked at Danny's reins to bring him into line. Behind her, Britt

68

had to pull Coconut up sharply to avoid running over Danny's heels, and Veronica shot her an irritated glance. "Careful! Can't you even keep your horse in line?" she hissed, loud enough for Stevie to hear. Stevie was also close enough to see Britt's face as it turned bright red. But the new girl didn't say a word in response to Veronica's unfair comment.

Meanwhile, Max had turned away from Veronica to survey the other students. "Any other questions? No? Good. Then let's see you keep those hands steady and backs straight."

Across the ring from Stevie, Carole and Lisa exchanged bemused glances. Stevie had filled them in on the situation before class, but they weren't surprised that the rest of their classmates were confused.

Max watched the class critically for a moment, then rode over to Simon Atherton, one of the weaker riders, to help him adjust his position. While he was busy, a few of the riders started to whisper to each other despite Max's strict no-talking-in-class rule.

"What do you think Max is doing?" Anna McWhirter whispered to Lisa. "I thought we'd be practicing gymkhana skills today."

Lisa just shrugged and smiled. She was almost as surprised as Anna herself, though not for the same reason. *She* couldn't believe that Max had actually given in to Stevie's wacky request. "That's Max," she said. "Always unpredictable."

* * *

AS SOON AS Max dismissed the class, Stevie dismounted and led Belle toward the bleachers, where her family was sitting.

"How did you like the lesson, Grandma?" she asked.

Grandma Lake walked forward to meet the girl and her horse. "This must be Belle!" she exclaimed. She reached out to stroke the mare's nose. "I've heard so much about her."

Stevie held her breath. Belle had a friendly temperament, but she could be feisty and playful. Stevie hoped the horse wouldn't frighten her grandmother. Fortunately, Belle seemed tired from the lesson and stood calmly while Grandma Lake patted her.

"What a lovely horse," Grandma Lake said sincerely. She glanced at Stevie's brothers, who were waiting nearby. "Don't you think so, boys?"

Alex started to make a face, but Chad elbowed him in the ribs. "Oops, sorry," Chad said sweetly. "Did I accidentally hit you, Alex?"

Alex frowned and rubbed his side. "Uh, no problem, Chad," he said. "It's quite all right."

Stevie bit back a laugh. Normally she preferred to keep her brothers far, far away from Pine Hollow. But it was kind of fun watching them try to be polite when she was sure that inside they were all dying to make fun of everything—especially her.

Stevie noticed Carole and Lisa heading toward the exit

and waved them over. "I want you to meet my two best friends, Grandma," she said. She introduced Carole, Lisa, and their horses.

"It's so nice to meet both of you," Grandma Lake said, smiling at the two girls. "I've heard almost as much about you as I have about Belle."

Carole and Lisa grinned. "Speaking of Belle," Lisa said, "do you want us to take care of her for you so you can show your grandmother around, Stevie?"

"Oh, a tour!" Grandma Lake exclaimed. "What a wonderful idea. I'd love to see the rest of this place, Stevie."

"Uh, thanks, guys," Stevie muttered. A tour? How could Lisa suggest such a thing? Still, Stevie reminded herself, the last thing she wanted to do was let her grandmother wander around by herself while she was busy untacking Belle. Who knew what kind of trouble she could get into that way? It would be better if Stevie took her for a quick look around the stable. Maybe then she would be satisfied and ready to depart for a nice, safe, soothing restaurant.

Once her friends had departed with Belle, Stevie took her grandmother by the arm and steered her toward the door. "Come on," she said. "I'll give you my special guided tour. Then we can go to dinner."

"Uh, we'll skip the tour," Alex spoke up quickly. "We've seen it already." Chad and Michael nodded.

Stevie smiled at them sweetly. "Are you sure?" she said. "Oh well, your loss."

Stevie's parents also decided to wait for Stevie and

Grandma Lake in the entry area. "Don't be long," Mrs. Lake warned. "We have reservations at the Willow Creek Inn in thirty minutes. And you still have to change clothes."

"Don't worry, Mom," Stevie said. As far as she was concerned, this was going to be the shortest Pine Hollow tour in history. All she wanted to do was get her grandmother out of there before anything bad happened to her, like tripping on something or getting nipped by a horse.

As she led her grandmother around the stable, Stevie was careful to introduce her to only the calmest horses. Grandma Lake met Nero, the oldest horse in the stable. She met the calm, gentle gelding named Patch, the horse Max usually assigned to beginning riders. She met a few of the ponies ridden by the youngest students. She met Veronica's horse, Danny, who was athletic and fiery in the ring but aloof and very sedate in his stall.

Stevie moved her grandmother past some stalls quickly. A few horses she avoided entirely, including Geronimo, Pine Hollow's resident stallion. Like many stallions, Geronimo could be unpredictable or even aggressive, especially with strangers. Stevie also skipped Magoo's stall, moving quickly from Danny's to another across the aisle. She was afraid that the sight of all those bandages would disturb Grandma Lake.

They had just reached Coconut's stall when Stevie spotted Polly Giacomin heading toward the tack room. "Um, I just remembered something," she said. "Can you

72

find your way back to the entry, Grandma? I think you've seen just about everything now."

"Sure, Stevie," Grandma Lake said, rubbing Coconut under the chin as the friendly gelding sighed with pleasure. "I'll be fine. Go ahead."

"Thanks." Stevie took off after Polly.

A few minutes later, everything was set. Polly was waiting in the locker room. Now all Stevie had to do was find Britt.

She found her leaning on the half door of Magoo's stall. As soon as she saw her there, Stevie smiled to herself. Obviously Lisa had been right. Britt really was trying to befriend The Saddle Club. She must have thought she'd find them taking care of Magoo as usual.

"Hi, Britt," Stevie said. "Um, I wonder if I could ask you a favor?"

"Sure," Britt said. "What is it? Do you need me to help you with Magoo again?"

"No, no, don't worry," Stevie assured her. "It's nothing like that." She grabbed the girl by the arm and dragged her toward the locker room. "You see, I'm supposed to go to dinner with my family now. But I forgot that I promised Polly I'd go with her to look at Romeo's brother. She really wanted someone to keep her company. Would you mind going in my place?"

Britt looked uncertain. "Are you sure? I don't know if she would want me to . . . ," she began.

By now they were entering the locker room. Polly

73

stood up when she saw them. "Hi, Britt," she said. "Did Stevie tell you what's going on? I hope you can come with me. I really want a second opinion on this horse before I start telling people about him."

Britt shrugged, still looking a little confused. "Um, okay," she said. "Just let me call my mom and tell her where I'm going."

"Great," Polly said. She followed Britt toward the door, tossing Stevie a wink on her way. "I'll come with you to the phone."

Stevie watched them go with a smile. Her plan was going perfectly. She had worked out the story with Polly. Now Polly and Britt were going to go see Romeo's brother—who just might possibly be Britt's dream horse. Stevie only wished she could go with them.

That reminded her that her family was waiting for her. She quickly changed out of her riding clothes, then hurried to the entryway. Grandma Lake was there chatting with Mrs. Reg. Both women were smiling and laughing and talking animatedly. They really seemed to be enjoying each other's company, which surprised Stevie. They didn't seem like the same type of person at all. Mrs. Reg was so brisk and lively and smart and hardworking. And Grandma Lake was so . . . well, old. What could they possibly have to talk about?

As Stevie came a little closer, she suddenly realized what the two women were talking about. The gymkhana!

"I do hope you can make it," Mrs. Reg was saying. "It

74

promises to be a lot of fun. Not to mention a lot of laughs."

"It sounds wonderful," Grandma Lake said warmly. "I wouldn't miss it for the world. I'm just surprised Stevie hadn't mentioned it to me yet." Just then she spotted Stevie. "Oh, hello, dear. We were just talking about your show on Saturday." She glanced at Mrs. Reg. "What did you call it again?"

Stevie answered for her. "A gymkhana," she said glumly. Her heart sank. What was she going to do now?

"DID YOU SEE Alex's face when his grandmother asked him what he thought of Belle?" Lisa giggled at the memory as she carefully examined Magoo's injured hock.

Carole laughed, too. "I never thought I'd see the day when Stevie's brothers would work so hard to be polite around here," she said. "You could tell they were itching to make fun of everything like they usually do. But instead they had to pretend to be interested."

Lisa started to rewrap Magoo's hock with a fresh bandage. "I wonder what Stevie's going to do about the gymkhana," she said. On her way out a few minutes earlier, Stevie had huddled with her friends long enough to tell them about her grandmother's plan to attend Saturday's event.

"I don't know," Carole said. "If she needs to avoid excitement, the gymkhana is the last place she should be. I hope Stevie can change her mind. And speaking of

75

changing people's minds," she added, "have you changed your mind about Coconut yet? He and Britt got along great in class today, didn't they?"

Lisa had to admit that they had. "Still," she argued, "Britt gets along great with every horse she meets." She gestured to Magoo. "Even this one seems to like her. She's totally horse-crazy. Isn't that one reason we're thinking about asking her to join The Saddle Club?"

"Does that mean you haven't given up on Applesauce yet?" Carole asked with a grin.

"No way," Lisa replied. "By the way, what do you think of Stevie's candidate?"

"You mean Romeo's half brother?" Carole asked. Stevie had also filled them in on her plan to send Britt with Polly. "Actually, I've seen him. Judy is his vet." Carole volunteered as a part-time assistant with the vet and sometimes accompanied her on her rounds. "He's no Coconut, but he is a really nice horse. He reminds me a lot of Romeo."

Magoo coughed. Lisa gave him a dirty look. "Stop that," she scolded the horse. "You know your cold is getting better. Judy said so this morning. Now you're just faking it to get attention."

"That's the least of his problems," Carole said. She gestured toward the wooden door of the stall. When the girls had entered that day, they had immediately noticed signs that Magoo had been cribbing—gnawing on the wood of the stall out of boredom. It was a bad habit, and one that the girls wanted to discourage immediately before Magoo started doing it all the time.

"I think he's just mad because he thinks we haven't been fussing over him enough," Lisa said. She shrugged. "Although yesterday we were in here for ages with Britt."

"Whatever the reason, we've got to nip this new cribbing habit in the bud," Carole said, giving Magoo a thoughtful look.

The horse stared back. Then, as if defying Carole to stop him, he reached over her shoulder and started to nibble on the stall door.

Lisa couldn't help laughing at the annoyed look on her friend's face. She stood up and gave Magoo a pat. "At least you admit you have a problem, right boy?"

"I think his main problem is that he's bored," Carole said. She patted Magoo, too. "He seems to need a lot more attention than the average horse. And I'm sure being cooped up in this stall and hardly getting any exercise while his injuries are healing isn't helping his state of mind."

"So what should we do?" Lisa asked.

Carole shrugged. "Obviously, the best thing would be to spend lots more time with him," she said. "But we can't do that without neglecting our own horses."

"Not to mention our families," Lisa agreed with a laugh. "And our homework, once school starts next week. And our sleep." She rubbed Magoo's nose. "He needs a *lot* of attention." Suddenly she had an idea. "Hey, doesn't

Max have one of those cribbing straps? I saw it in the tack room the other day."

Carole nodded. "He used it to break that boarder of the habit last year," she said. "But that horse was a die-hard cribber. Magoo doesn't have that big a problem yet, so the strap seems kind of extreme to me."

The cribbing strap Lisa was talking about was a leather device that prevented a horse's neck from expanding, stopping the intake of air that accompanied cribbing. As far as Carole knew, Max had used it only once, on a horse with a very serious problem. She didn't think he would approve of its use on Magoo. But what else could they try, short of moving cots into his stall and holding his hoof full-time?

"I've got it!" she cried suddenly. "Veronica!"

Lisa cocked her head to one side and gave her friend a curious look. "Veronica?" she said. "What does she know about cribbing? Danny doesn't have a single bad habit that I know of."

"That's exactly the point," Carole said. She let herself out of the stall and motioned for Lisa to follow. "Veronica just bought Danny all those expensive horse toys for Christmas, remember? And I don't think he's so much as glanced at any of them."

Lisa's eyes widened. "I get it!" she said. "Those kinds of toys are meant to keep horses occupied while they're in their stalls. To keep them from developing bad habits, like wind sucking or weaving or—"

78

"Cribbing," Carole finished for her with a nod.

"But doesn't that mean we have to ask Veronica to loan them to us?" Lisa said, wrinkling her nose in distaste. "She might not let us use them. She kept bragging about the expensive catalog she ordered them from."

Carole shrugged. "All we can do is ask, right?"

The girls left the stall and went in search of Veronica. "I hope she didn't leave already," Lisa said as she peeked into the student locker room. Veronica was famous for expecting Red and the other stable hands to do her work for her. It wouldn't be unusual for her to have left the stable, even so soon after class.

But the girls were lucky. As they headed toward the tack room, they heard voices coming from Mrs. Reg's office. One of the voices was very loud, very whiny, and very familiar.

Carole poked her head through the door. She saw Max perched on the edge of his mother's desk, looking irritated. Veronica was standing in front of him, hands on her hips, complaining.

"But Max," she whined, not noticing Carole. "You promised we could play the shopping game I made up!"

Max sighed. "I told you we could do it if you agreed to supply the props," he reminded Veronica.

"But I just told you," Veronica said, pouting. "I don't have time to make all that stuff this week. I've got a lot to do."

"Well, you're welcome to do it next week," Max said

with a shrug, "but that won't help us much, since the gymkhana is this Saturday."

Carole knocked softly on the doorjamb to announce her presence. "Sorry to interrupt," she said, "but we have a question—for both of you, actually." She came into the office, followed by Lisa.

Max nodded. Carole thought he looked a little relieved to have this particular conversation interrupted. "Go ahead, Carole," he said.

Carole told him about Magoo's new cribbing problem. Then she explained the solution she and Lisa were considering.

Max looked thoughtful. "I've noticed that Magoo is quite demanding of human attention. I don't know if toys will be an adequate substitute for him. But it's certainly worth a try if Veronica is willing to lend them to you."

Veronica was already frowning. "What makes you think I want some strange horse slobbering all over my Danny's things?" she demanded, turning to face Carole and Lisa. "That horse doesn't even belong to Pine Hollow. Besides that, he's disruptive. He's always staring at me when I go by and making noise when I'm in Danny's stall."

Lisa rolled her eyes, but she tried to be polite when she answered. After all, they needed Veronica's help. "That's why we need the toys," she said as patiently as she could. "We're hoping they'll keep him occupied so that he won't be so restless. We'll take good care of them and return them as soon as Magoo goes home to Hedgerow. We promise."

Veronica still looked stubborn. She shook her head and started to reply.

Carole interrupted. "I've got an idea," she said suddenly. "Why don't we make a deal?"

Veronica closed her mouth and looked suspicious. "What kind of deal?" she asked. Max didn't say anything, but he looked interested.

"If you'll lend us one of your horse toys," Carole said, "we'll make the props for your shopping game before the gymkhana." She gestured to Lisa, who looked surprised but nodded quickly.

Veronica thought it over for a second. "All right," she said at last. "It's a deal. Okay, Max? If they make the props, is my game in?" When Max nodded, Veronica turned back to the other two girls. "That means you'll have to gather some stuff to use for merchandise and make receipts and signs for each store."

"Fine," Lisa said. "We can handle that."

Veronica wasn't finished. "*I'll* supply the shopping bags, though," she said, brushing a bit of lint off her immaculate, expensive-looking breeches. She tipped her head up and looked down her nose at Carole and Lisa. "After all, you two probably don't frequent the kinds of shops I want represented in *my* game."

"THANKS FOR COMING with me, Britt," Lisa said the next afternoon. She and Britt were once again walking up Hedgerow's curving driveway. "I really wanted to come back and visit again, and Carole and Stevie couldn't come with me."

Britt shrugged and smiled shyly. "I guess I'm the designated fill-in," she said. "Yesterday I went to visit a horse with Polly because Stevie couldn't do it."

Lisa frowned at the mention of Britt's trip with Polly. "Oh, right," she said, trying to sound casual. "Stevie mentioned something about that."

"Romeo's brother looks a lot like him, except he's bay instead of brown," Britt said. "He seemed like a really nice horse."

Normally that wouldn't sound like a very strong recommendation. But Lisa knew that with Britt it was hard to tell. She hoped that the fact that Britt had brought up the topic without being prompted didn't mean that she was really interested in Romeo's half brother.

Still, Lisa wasn't too worried. She'd arranged for Britt to ride Applesauce during today's visit to Hedgerow. And once that happened, Britt was sure to fall in love with the sweet-tempered mare. Lisa just hoped that Elaine had filled in her head groom as promised. The ride had to seem like a spur-of-the-moment idea, or Britt might catch on and the surprise would be ruined.

"THEY'RE LATE," STEVIE said, glancing at her watch.

Carole drummed her spoon on the table. The two girls were sitting in their favorite booth at TD's, an ice cream parlor at a shopping center near Pine Hollow. "I know," she said. "I wonder if that means she can't bear to tear herself away from Applesauce."

Earlier in the day, The Saddle Club had arranged to meet at TD's. Lisa was supposed to bring Britt along after their trip to Hedgerow. It was all part of the plan to befriend Britt and, if all went well, ask her to join The Saddle Club.

Stevie rested her head on one hand and gazed at the empty seat across from her and Carole. "You know, I never noticed it before," she mused. "The three of us almost always sit in this booth. But it's really a table built for four. Do you think that's some kind of sign?"

"I don't know about that," Carole said. "I think a better sign is the fact that Britt fits our requirements so well. So far she's always seemed willing to help us out, no matter what we ask her to do."

"True," Stevie agreed. "She even pitches in to help with Magoo the medical monster without complaining at all."

Carole nodded. "And we already know she's completely horse-crazy," she said. She wasn't wearing a watch, so she grabbed Stevie's arm to check hers. "I just wonder if she's becoming crazy about one particular horse right now."

At that moment, the small bell above the shop's door tinkled softly. Carole and Stevie looked up and saw Lisa and Britt entering.

Soon all four girls were seated. The waitress brought them glasses of water. "I'll be back to take your order in a second," she said, giving Stevie a noticeably sour look.

"What was that all about?" Britt whispered as the woman stalked away.

Lisa giggled. "She's not very fond of Stevie," she explained. "You'll understand why in a minute." Stevie always ordered outrageous combinations of ice cream and toppings at TD's.

"Actually, I don't have much of an appetite today,"

Stevie admitted. "I might only be able to manage a little pistachio ice cream with strawberry sauce."

Britt wrinkled her nose, but Carole and Lisa looked concerned. "Are you worrying about your grandmother?" Carole asked.

Stevie nodded and started drumming her spoon against her water glass, almost tipping it over. "I've got to talk her out of coming to the gymkhana," she said.

Lisa reached across the table and rescued Stevie's water glass. "That's the best plan," she agreed. "You may have convinced Max to calm down our class yesterday, but that won't work with the gymkhana."

Britt was starting to look confused. The other girls quickly filled her in on the situation with Stevie's grandmother.

"The worst part is, it's getting harder and harder for my brothers and me to keep up the act," Stevie said with a sigh. "It's kind of weird. Our house is so quiet and peaceful now that it doesn't even seem like home anymore. I never realized how much fighting with my brothers and making their lives miserable means to me. But it's important to keep things calm for Grandma, so I'm doing my best." She sighed again, more deeply this time.

Carole decided it was time for a change of subject. "By the way," she said, "did you all notice that Magoo hasn't been cribbing since we gave him that horse toy?" As promised, Veronica had lent them one of Danny's toys, a

85

large plastic one almost a foot in diameter that looked and smelled like a giant apple. The girls had hung it from the roof of Magoo's stall with a thick rope so that the horse could play with it safely.

"He did start fussing with his bandages again, though," Lisa pointed out. "Every time he nibbles at one, the hot sauce burns his mouth and he starts jumping around."

"I know," Carole said worriedly. "Max is afraid he'll hurt himself, and so am I. We'll have to figure out a better way to get him to leave the bandages alone."

Britt cleared her throat. "Um, I have a couple of ideas if you want to hear them," she said.

"Of course we do," Stevie said. "What are they?"

Once three pairs of eyes were trained expectantly on her, Britt started to look a little nervous. But she cleared her throat again and spoke. "There was a horse at my old stable who had the same problem," she said. "They tried cayenne pepper on the bandages, but it didn't seem to bother him." She grinned. "My old instructor said it was because he was part Paso Fino and so he liked spicy food."

The other girls laughed at that. Paso Finos were Spanish in origin. "So, what happened?" Lisa asked.

"First they tried a neck cradle," Britt said.

"Oh, of course! Why didn't I think of that?" Carole exclaimed. A neck cradle was a common piece of protective equipment, useful for keeping a horse from removing blankets or bandages. "I know Max has one around somewhere."

Britt shrugged. "They're not foolproof, though," she warned. "It didn't work on this horse. He almost went crazy when they made him wear it. They were afraid he was going to hurt himself more by trying to get it off than he would by ripping off his bandages. He really hated having his head movement limited that way." She giggled. "And Magoo really has a mind of his own. I have a feeling he might react the same way."

"You're probably right about that," Stevie agreed.

"Next, they tried cross-tying him while he was alone in his stall," Britt said. "He hated that almost as much. Luckily, the next thing they tried worked. They attached a leather bib to his halter. That did the trick.

Carole nodded thoughtfully. Britt had come up with some good suggestions for them to try. But more important in a way, she had just demonstrated once again why she was truly Saddle Club material. Her interest in horses and willingness to help had just intersected. Although she didn't realize it, Britt had just fulfilled both of their club's rules at once!

Lisa was thinking about something else. "Guess what," she told Carole and Stevie, trying her best to sound casual. "Britt rode that Hedgerow mare Applesauce today."

"Really?" Stevie said, playing along. "How come?"

Britt took a sip of water. "The groom asked me to," she said. "He said she'd just been reshod and he was worried that one of the new shoes was bothering her. He wanted

someone to put her through her paces while he watched."
She shrugged. "But she turned out to be fine."

Carole and Stevie exchanged amused glances. Britt
didn't sound suspicious at all, even though the story was
pretty lame.

"Britt thought Applesauce had really nice gaits," Lisa
put in, looking very pleased with herself. As she had
guessed, Britt had seemed to like the mare a lot. "Didn't
you, Britt?"

Britt nodded. "She's a really nice horse," she said,
sounding a little distracted. "Hey, isn't that Polly walking
by out there?"

Lisa twisted around in the seat to look. She was just in
time to see Polly stroll past on the walkway outside the
glass door of the restaurant. "That's her," she said.

Britt quickly scooted out of the booth. "Um, I think I'll
go catch up to her," she said. "She lives down the street
from me, and maybe I can get a ride home with her if
she's leaving soon. Otherwise I'll have to take the bus. My
mom's working late." She gave The Saddle Club an anxious glance. "You don't mind, do you?"

"Go ahead," Stevie assured her. "We'll forgive you if
you eat and run this time. Even though you didn't even
eat."

Britt looked relieved. "Thanks," she said with a smile.
She hurried away. A moment later, with a tinkling of the
bell on the door, she was gone.

"It's too bad she couldn't stay longer," Lisa said.

Carole shrugged. "I know how she feels," she said. "Taking the bus is a pain in the neck, especially when it's cold outside." Unlike her friends, Carole lived too far from Pine Hollow to walk home. She had to take the town bus whenever she couldn't get a ride from her father or another rider's parents.

"Besides," Stevie pointed out, just as the waitress reluctantly stopped in front of their table again and pulled out her order pad, "we'll have plenty of time to spend with Britt once she joins The Saddle Club."

"DID YOU GIVE Max our list of ideas?" Carole asked.

Lisa nodded. Then, realizing that Carole couldn't see her over the phone, she added, "Yep. He thought there were some good ones." After Britt had left the ice cream shop that day, the other girls had spent some time thinking up more ideas for the gymkhana. Lisa had promised to stop by the stable on her way home and give them to Max. "He especially liked the costume relay where the horses get dressed up instead of the riders."

Carole giggled. "That's my favorite, too," she said. "It will—" She paused as a soft tone sounded on the line. "Is that your call waiting?"

"I think so," Lisa said. "Hold on a second." She put Carole on hold and pressed the button to pick up the other call. "Hello? Atwood residence, Lisa speaking."

"Hi, Lisa," said a cheerful woman's voice. "This is Joanne Lynn."

"Oh, hi," Lisa greeted Britt's mother. "I was just talking to Carole on the other line."

"Oh, sorry," the woman said. "I won't keep you long. I just wanted to call and thank you for spending so much time with Britt lately. She really enjoyed visiting that other stable with you today."

Lisa smiled. "I had fun, too," she said. "Did Britt tell you she got to ride one of the horses?"

"She sure did." Ms. Lynn lowered her voice a little. "That reminds me, I also wanted to thank you and your friends for all your help on our little project," she said. "From everything she's said to me, it sounds like she's already picked out the horse she wants, even if she doesn't know yet that she's getting one."

Lisa's heart jumped with excitement. She had been right! Britt really had fallen in love with Applesauce! "That's great," Lisa said. She was about to press for details, but Ms. Lynn spoke up before she could.

"I'll let you get back to your other call now," the woman said. "Maybe we can talk more at your show on Saturday. I'll be coming to watch, of course."

"Great," Lisa said. "See you then."

She said good-bye and pressed the button to switch the line back to the original call. *Just wait until Carole hears about this!*

STEVIE LOOKED UP as Lisa entered the student locker room
the next day. "Got everything?" she asked.

Lisa nodded and held up a pair of scissors. "I borrowed
these from Mrs. Reg," she said. "Carole is coming with
the props. She went to find Britt and ask if she wants to
help out."

Stevie gestured to the piece of construction paper on
the bench in front of her. "I've got most of the front parts
of the receipts done," she said. She was writing names of
various items in large letters, making "receipts" that were
half a page in size. "All I have to do now is cut them out
and then add the names of the stores on the back—if
Veronica ever shows up with those shopping bags, that
is."

"She said she'd be here," Lisa said, glancing at her watch. "If she doesn't show up soon, maybe we can try calling her. We have to get this stuff done fast—the gymkhana is the day after tomorrow."

"I know," Stevie said. "And I promised my parents I'd hang around at home tomorrow and spend some time with Grandma, so I won't be able to help you if we don't finish today."

Just then Carole hurried into the room. She was carrying a boxful of small pieces of tack, assorted grooming tools, and other items, which would serve as "merchandise" for the game. "How's it going?" she asked.

The others told her. "I'm just about to start making the signs that will mark the location of each store," Lisa added, grabbing a brightly colored marking pen from the pile on the floor next to Stevie. "I won't be able to add the names until Veronica brings us the bags—she wants them to match—but I thought I'd draw some borders and things to make them look nice."

"Where's Britt?" Stevie asked.

Carole set the box on the bench. "She begged off," she said. "She told me she'd help if we really needed her, but she wanted to put in some extra practice on Coconut since she'll be riding him in the games on Saturday." She grinned triumphantly. "Naturally, I told her to go ahead."

"I don't know what you're looking so smug about," Lisa said. "Ms. Lynn told me that Britt already decided she likes Applesauce best." She paused, thinking back on the

92

phone conversation. "At least, I thought that was what she said."

Stevie shrugged. "Who knows?" she said. "Maybe she's still making up her mind. For one thing, she doesn't even know that she's actually getting a horse."

"True," Carole said. "Besides, it's a really big decision. She needs to be really sure, and that means exploring all her options carefully." She smiled. "I can't wait to see her face when she finds out her mom is getting her another horse. I still remember how thrilled I was when Dad surprised me with Starlight." That had been one of the best moments of her life, and she was glad Britt would get to experience something similar. She could practically picture Britt's shining face as she hugged Coconut for the first time after realizing that he was hers forever.

Stevie nodded. She was remembering her own feelings when she had gotten Belle. "It will be great," she said dreamily, imagining Britt's response when presented with Romeo's lively, wonderful half brother for her very own.

Lisa didn't have her own horse yet, but she would never forget the day that Prancer had come to live at Pine Hollow. Lisa had fallen in love with the lovely Thoroughbred from the first time she saw her. She knew it would be even more special for Britt when she brought her own mare, Applesauce, to live at Pine Hollow.

Carole sighed deeply. "It's going to be wonderful for her, no matter which horse she chooses," she said. "I just hope that after that, being asked to join The Saddle Club won't seem anticlimactic."

"Never," Lisa said loyally.

But Stevie had a very funny look on her face. "I just remembered something," she said. "Speaking of asking Britt things, has any of us asked her to be on our team for the gymkhana yet?"

Both her friends shook their heads. "I forgot," Carole said.

"Me too," Lisa added. "Poor Britt. I hope she doesn't think she's going to be without a team on Saturday."

Stevie capped the black marker she was using and tossed it on the pile. "I keep forgetting to mention it, too," she said. "I guess I've been distracted by all the excitement of Grandma's visit." She sighed. "Or maybe I should say all the *non*-excitement."

Carole grinned. "Does this mean your temporary truce with your brothers is still holding?"

"You bet," Stevie said. "My house has never been so quiet and sedate. Mom and Dad can't figure out what happened, but they're not complaining." She snorted. "Although I find it hard to believe that anyone could actually *prefer* things so boring."

Lisa looked up from the sign she was making and laughed. "Oh, I don't know," she said. "I'll bet my mom would prefer it, too." Lisa's mother was famous for liking things quiet, orderly, and genteel.

Quiet, orderly, and *genteel* were usually the last three words anyone would use to describe Stevie's house. But these days they actually fit. "I'm just glad we only have to keep it up for another week," Stevie said. "It's nice to know we have enough self-control and restraint to make it work. But if Grandma were staying any longer than two weeks, I just might explode!"

At that moment Veronica came stomping into the room. "There you are!" she exclaimed when she saw The Saddle Club. "I was looking all over for you."

"We told you we'd be here," Carole said. "Did you bring the bags?"

Veronica stared at her blankly for a second. "What?" she snapped. Then she realized what Carole was talking about. "Oh, those. They're in my cubby." She waved her hand vaguely toward the wall of cubbyholes where students stored their things while they were riding. "But never mind that right now. You've got to do something about that stupid horse. He's out of control."

Carole had already started toward Veronica's cubby to retrieve the shopping bags, but she stopped short and turned around. "What horse?" she asked. "Do you mean Magoo?"

"Of course I do." Veronica tossed her head. "He's making such a fuss that it's starting to upset Danny. I don't want him to get all excited and worn out before the gymkhana, or he won't be at his peak."

Carole, Lisa, and Stevie exchanged anxious glances. None of them was the least bit concerned about Danny. They all knew that nothing short of an explosion in his stall would disturb the imperturbable gelding. But they were all worried about Magoo. What was he up to now?

They hurried out of the room after Veronica to find out. When they reached Magoo's stall, they found the chestnut gelding standing with his head hanging out over the half door, snorting loudly and swinging his neck from side to side. As they watched, he backed into his stall. A moment later they heard the sound of his hoofs against the side wall.

"See what I mean?" Veronica demanded. "Poor Danny!" She rushed over to her horse's stall and let herself in.

Carole glanced in at Danny. As expected, he was standing impassively near the front, munching on a mouthful of hay. She turned her attention to Magoo.

Lisa was already at the gelding's head, soothing him while Stevie examined him. "He ripped off a few more bandages," Stevie reported.

Carole could see that for herself. "It looks like the hot sauce is still making him nuts," she said. "We'll have to stop using it."

"Maybe we should try one of those suggestions Britt gave us yesterday," Lisa said.

Carole nodded. "I guess so," she said, "but we should probably talk to Max before we try anything too drastic."

"Let's go find him," Stevie said, heading out of the stall.

Veronica stuck her head out as the other girls walked past. "Aren't you going to do anything about that crazy horse?" she snapped. "He's a menace."

The Saddle Club girls didn't bother to answer.

They couldn't locate Max anywhere in the stable. Finally they found Red in the grain shed, and he told them that Max was out on the trail with an adult class. When he heard why they needed him, the stable hand suggested talking to Mrs. Reg. "She knows practically everything there is to know about the nutty things horses do," he said. "Besides, she's got all those reference books in her office. Maybe you can check out some methods in one of them."

"Great idea," Stevie said. "Thanks, Red."

The girls found Mrs. Reg in her office, working on some papers. When The Saddle Club entered, Mrs. Reg set down her pen and smiled at them. "What can I do for you three?" she asked.

Carole explained their mission. "We thought you might have some ideas," she said.

Mrs. Reg stood and pulled a thick reference book off the shelf behind her desk. "Let's take a quick look in here," she said, flipping to the index.

Meanwhile, Stevie glanced at her watch. "Rats," she muttered. "I've got to go soon. Grandma's taking me and my brothers to the movies."

"That doesn't sound like anything to complain about," Mrs. Reg commented, peering at Stevie over the top of the oversized book.

Stevie shrugged. "Normally it wouldn't be," she said. "But we're seeing that new foreign movie *Garden of Tranquillity*. It's all about some rose breeder from the nineteenth century. I heard there are only sixteen lines of dialogue in the entire movie—the rest just shows her digging around in the dirt and making flower arrangements and stuff. It sounds totally dull."

Mrs. Reg looked surprised. "Why are you seeing it, then?" she asked. "I'm sure your grandmother doesn't want to take you to a movie that's going to bore you." She laughed. "And I must admit, I'm having a hard time picturing you and your brothers sitting through a film like that."

Stevie shrugged. "We told her we wanted to see it," she admitted. "And it's not really a lie. We *did* want to make sure to see something that won't be too much for her."

"Too much for her?" Mrs. Reg repeated questioningly.

Stevie quickly explained her concerns about her grandmother's health.

"I see," Mrs. Reg said thoughtfully. "That explains things." She returned her attention to the book in front of her. "Now, let's see what we can do about Magoo's latest problem."

"Why do you think Magoo is so difficult, Mrs. Reg?"

Lisa asked, perching on the arm of a chair near the office door.

"Probably for the same reason some people are difficult," Mrs. Reg said. "No particular reason at all. He just likes a lot of attention and has figured out the best way to get it." She ran her finger down the index and then turned to another page.

"Did you find anything?" Stevie asked expectantly after a moment, glancing at her watch again.

"Not yet," Mrs. Reg said. She lowered the book once more and gazed at The Saddle Club. "Did I ever tell you the story of Little Red?"

All three girls shook their heads. Stevie sneaked another look at her watch. Mrs. Reg's stories were legendary. They always had a specific point, but it usually wasn't easy to recognize it at first. Most importantly, it was impossible to tell at the beginning of one how long it was going to be. Stevie was cutting things close as it was.

If Mrs. Reg noticed Stevie's concern, she didn't let on. "They called him Little Red because he was a little fellow, fourteen hands, two inches on the nose." That was the maximum height at which an animal would be properly known as a pony. "Because of his size, Max tried for a long time to use him with the younger students." The girls knew that the Max Mrs. Reg meant was the current Max's father, her late husband. "But Little Red was just too feisty for the beginners. Finally Max decided he would have to sell him. What could he do with a pony that wouldn't do a pony's job?"

She stopped talking. The girls waited for a moment. They knew that Mrs. Reg hated to be interrupted when she was telling a story. But when the woman started rustling through the pages of her book again, Carole couldn't resist. "Well? What happened?" she asked. "Did he sell Little Red?"

Mrs. Reg shrugged. "Of course he did," she said. "A buyer turned up almost immediately—a really petite teenager. She and Little Red won dozens of blue ribbons together in Open Jumper classes."

"Don't you mean the Hunter-Jumper Pony division?" Carole asked.

Mrs. Reg shook her head and smiled. "Nope," she said. "You see, Max's trouble was that he thought of Little Red as a pony. But Little Red thought of himself as a horse."

Stevie checked the time again. At least this story had been a short one. She had no idea what Little Red and his height delusions had to do with Magoo. And she didn't have time to try to figure it out. If they didn't solve Magoo's problem soon, she would have to leave her friends to deal with it without her.

Just then the phone rang. Mrs. Reg picked it up and listened for a moment, then asked the caller to hang on. "I've got to take this," she said, covering the mouthpiece with her hand. "All of your ideas to stop Magoo from removing his bandages sound reasonable to me. Why don't you take the book with you and see if you can figure out which method they suggest?"

As Mrs. Reg returned to her call, Lisa scooped up the heavy book and carried it out into the aisle. Moments later the three girls were back at Magoo's stall.

Lisa opened the book and quickly found the chapter on treating behavioral problems. "This book seems to think that leaving the horse in cross-ties when he's alone is the easiest and most effective method," she said after reading for a moment.

Stevie peered over her shoulder. "Really?" she said dubiously. "That's only because they don't know Magoo. I don't think he'll like that very much."

Carole glanced at the horse, who was watching them curiously over the stall door. "Who knows?" she said. "You never can tell how a horse will react to something until you try it."

That was good enough for Lisa. She slammed the big book shut. "Good," she said. "Cross-ties it is, then. We'll do it as soon as we repair the damage he's already done to his bandages."

Stevie gave her friends an apologetic look. "Listen, I'd love to help with that, but I've really got to go," she said. "Do you mind?"

"Of course not," Carole said. "Go ahead. You don't want to be late for the movie." She grinned. "I'd hate for you to miss the planting of the seeds at the beginning or anything. You might never figure out the rest of the plot."

Stevie stuck her tongue out at her. "Very funny," she said. "Just for that, I'm not even going to feel guilty about leaving you to finish Veronica's stupid props, too."

"Don't worry about a thing," Lisa said. "Maybe we can catch Britt when she's finished practicing. I'm sure she'll help out then."

"Good," Stevie said. She gave Magoo a good-bye pat on the nose and started to hurry away, but she stopped before she had gone more than half a dozen steps. Something had just occurred to her. She turned back to her friends. "Hey, did you ever wonder why Magoo is still here?" she asked. "I mean, I understand why Judy didn't want him moved at first, but he's really not in such bad shape anymore, especially these past few days. Elaine and her people at Hedgerow could deal with his fussiness just as well as we can—probably better. So why is he still here?"

Carole had wondered the same thing more than once in the past day or two, but she hadn't said anything about it. "I don't know," she admitted. "I'm sure Judy has her reasons."

Lisa nodded. "Or maybe Max and Elaine worked something out."

Stevie shrugged. "Okay," she said, turning to go. "I was just wondering, that's all."

". . . So do you see what I mean?" Stevie was saying the next day. "I just don't think you'd have a good time."

Her grandmother nodded thoughtfully and leaned back on the living room couch. "You've made some interesting points, Stevie," she said.

Stevie held her breath. She had pulled out all the stops to convince Grandma Lake that coming to the gymkhana the next day would be a mistake. She had checked the weather forecast and found out that Saturday would be cold and windy—perfect weather for staying in the nice, cozy house. She had carefully described how dusty the indoor ring could get, especially with a lot of horses and riders racing around in it. That was just terrible for the lungs. And she had explained that most of the games and races would be hard to follow if you hadn't seen a gymkhana before. In fact, the whole show would probably be downright boring for someone like Grandma Lake.

"I can tell that you have my best interests at heart, dear," Grandma Lake said. She picked up the deck of cards lying on the coffee table in front of her and started to shuffle them. Stevie's mother was in the kitchen making some tea and sandwiches. When they were ready, the three of them were going to play a few rounds of cards. Stevie was glad that they didn't have enough people for bridge. She had just learned to play, but she hated it already.

"I don't want you to be bored, that's all," Stevie assured her grandmother.

"I know that. And—" Grandma Lake was interrupted by a sudden loud commotion in the hallway. A second later Michael slid past the open doorway on his stomach, his arms stretched out in front of him, holding a baseball cap to the floor. Stevie frowned. What was her brother doing? Didn't he realize that their grandmother was in there?

"Stay right here, Grandma," she said. "I'll be right back." She jumped out of her chair and hurried into the hall. "What's going on out here?" she hissed.

Michael gazed up at her, still holding down the cap with both hands. "Sorry, Stevie," he whispered back,

104

panting a little. "I couldn't help it. Eenie and Meenie escaped. I had to catch them."

Stevie frowned and glanced at the cap. For the first time, she noticed that it appeared to be wriggling. "You mean your white mice are under there?" she demanded, still keeping her voice low. "Are you crazy? If Grandma sees those rodents on the loose, she'll have a heart attack!"

"I know," Michael said sorrowfully. "I didn't do it on purpose. I just opened the door of their cage to feed them, and they ran out."

Stevie scowled. "Well, put them back right now," she ordered him. "And if they get out again while Grandma's here, I'll sic Madonna on them."

Michael's eyes widened. Madonna was Stevie's cat. Without another word, he carefully gathered the two white mice in the cap and scurried for the stairs.

Stevie returned to the living room. "Sorry about that, Grandma," she said casually. "It was nothing to worry about. Michael just tripped." She sat down. "Now, where were we?"

"I was just saying how much I appreciate your concern for me," Grandma Lake said. "And I was going to go on to reassure you that I certainly don't want to do anything that will endanger my health."

"Really?" Stevie said. "Do you promise?"

"I promise," her grandmother said with a smile. "I have no intention of spending tomorrow morning bored stiff."

Stevie's mother hurried into the room with a tray full of food. "Here we go," she said. "This should hold us for a while. Tea, Stevie?"

Stevie nodded. She didn't really like tea, but at the moment she was so relieved that she would have gladly accepted a cup of hot bran mash to drink. She had done it! She had talked her grandmother out of coming to the gymkhana! Nothing else mattered—not even the coming boring afternoon of ladylike card playing and tea drinking.

Grandma Lake picked up the cards again and started to deal them out. "Let's play cards," she said. "How about a few hands of old maid?"

AT THE SAME time that Stevie was playing her first hand of old maid, Carole and Lisa were at Pine Hollow. Once again, they were standing in front of Magoo's stall, staring at him. Britt was with them. They had found her waiting for them there.

"Okay, so the cross-ties didn't work," Lisa said. "What's next?"

As soon as they had arrived at the stable that day, Red had given them the bad news. Magoo had tolerated the cross-ties for just over an hour after they had left. Then he had kicked up such a ruckus that Max had been forced to spend an hour calming him down.

Carole bit her lip. "I can't believe we have to replace all those bandages again," she said. The bandages were scattered all over the stall. Only a few remained on the horse.

"Don't worry," Britt said quietly. She reached for the latch on the stall door. "I'll take care of it this time if you want."

That made Carole and Lisa forget their irritation with Magoo. They exchanged yet another of the secret smiles that were becoming so frequent lately. The more time they spent with Britt, the more certain they were. She was definitely Saddle Club material. She fulfilled both rules every day without even realizing it. And even if she hadn't yet opened up with them as much as they would like, the girls were sure that she would in time.

"Thanks, Britt," Lisa said. "That's really helpful of you. I'm afraid I'm starting to lose some patience with our patient." She giggled. "Get it? *Patience* with the *patient?*"

Britt smiled slightly, but she didn't really look amused. "Magoo can't help it," she said. "He doesn't understand why the bandages have to stay on. Besides, he's just doing it because he's restless and bored after being cooped up so long."

Carole nodded, immediately feeling bad about her own attitude, which was much the same as Lisa's. "You're right, Britt," she said. "Magoo is a horse, not a person. He doesn't understand why he has to stay in his stall so much these days. And he doesn't know any better way to express how frustrated he is."

Britt smiled at Carole, then at Lisa. "Sorry," she said

softly. "I didn't mean to scold you guys. I just feel bad that Magoo is so lonely and unhappy."

Lisa wondered if Britt could empathize with the horse's loneliness because she was lonely herself. It wouldn't be surprising. Being new in town was hard for anyone, and for shy Britt it must be excruciating.

But The Saddle Club would fix that soon, Lisa reminded herself. Once Britt joined, she wouldn't ever have to be lonely and unhappy again. "Come on," she said, letting herself into the stall. "Let's get Magoo fixed up. It won't take long if we all work together."

LATER, CAROLE CAUGHT UP to Lisa in the tack room. Nobody else was there, so she sat down to talk. "This all feels really right, doesn't it?" she said.

Lisa nodded. She didn't even have to ask what Carole was referring to. "At first it seemed weird to even think about adding a fourth full-time member," she said, scrubbing slowly at Prancer's saddle. "It's always been just the three of us—ever since the beginning. But Britt fits so well."

"And I think she'll be thrilled when we ask her," Carole said. "Lately it seems like she's finding any excuse to hang out with us. She obviously wants to be our friend."

Lisa grinned. "Who can blame her?" She gave the saddle one last swipe, then tossed her sponge into a nearby bucket and stood up. "I'm finished here. Are you ready to go?"

The girls left the tack room and headed for the door. On the way, they passed the door to the indoor ring. It was propped open, and they could see Britt inside, mounted on Coconut.

"Let's stop in and say good-bye," Carole suggested. She and Lisa stepped through the doorway and called to Britt.

Britt turned to look at them. So did two other riders, who had been hidden from view until the girls had entered the ring.

"Hi, guys," said Polly. "What's up?"

"Oh, hi, Polly," Lisa said. "Hi, Lorraine."

Lorraine smiled. "Are you as excited about the gymkhana as we are?" she asked.

"More," Carole assured her with a grin. "It's going to be fun."

Polly gathered up her reins as Romeo tossed his head. "Max said we're going to have to ask our horses to back up in one of the races, so we decided we'd better practice. Britt's helping us."

Lorraine nodded enthusiastically. "She's been a huge help," she said. "She's really good. I've never seen Coconut perform so well!"

"It was nothing," Britt said, blushing. "Coconut did all the work. I just sat there."

"You're too modest, Britt," Polly said. "Now come on. You promised to help me get Romeo to back up in a straight line instead of curving off to the side."

Carole and Lisa said good-bye to all three of the other

109

girls and left. "Isn't that great?" Lisa asked once they were out of earshot. "Britt's really coming out of her shell!"

"And it's all thanks to us," Carole said proudly. "She's really got that Saddle Club spirit. By the way, did you notice how great she and Coconut were doing—again?" She grinned. "It's like they were meant to be together."

Lisa smiled back. She didn't necessarily agree with that, but she didn't feel like arguing at the moment. "Right," she said, linking her arm through Carole's. "Just like The Saddle Club."

"I CAN'T BELIEVE we forgot to ask her yesterday," Lisa said as she and Carole hurried toward Magoo's stall the next morning.

Carole shot her an exasperated glance. "Would you stop worrying?" she said. "We'll ask her as soon as she gets here. It will be fine. What other team would Britt expect to be on but ours?"

"But she's so insecure," Lisa said. "What if she's been worrying all week because we haven't asked her yet? Maybe she thinks we don't want her on our team." She had been thinking similar kinds of thoughts all night, ever since the moment at dinner when she had realized that The Saddle Club still hadn't asked Britt to be on their team for the gymkhana. After dinner she had tried to call the Lynns' house, but nobody had answered. Now the day of the gymkhana was here, and Lisa felt terrible at the thought that they might have unintentionally put their new friend through days of misery.

Carole stopped in front of Magoo's stall. As soon as she saw the horse, she frowned. Magoo was at the front of the stall. He tossed his head and snorted when he saw the girls. Then he backed away and stamped his feet. He tossed his head again and circled around in the stall a couple of times. Then he returned to the front and peered out over the door again.

"He seems pretty agitated," Lisa said. "Do you think something else is wrong with him?"

"I don't know," Carole replied. She watched Magoo silently for another minute or two. The horse continued to seem upset, but Carole couldn't see any obvious signs of colic or any other problem. "Maybe he's just feeling lonely again. Let's see if our company helps."

The girls went into the stall to check on Magoo's bandages. Despite their presence, the horse continued to seem worked up and edgy. "You know, normally I feel sorry for any horse that's upset," Lisa said as she dodged aside to avoid having Magoo step on her foot. "But I still can't help thinking he's doing it on purpose."

"I know," Carole said. "Maybe that's why Elaine is so eager to sell him. He's no good in a big stable. He needs an owner that will pay attention to him and baby him twenty-four hours a day."

Lisa moved aside again as Magoo pushed past her on his way to the front of the stall. "Maybe," she agreed with a rueful smile. "But I'm not going to volunteer for *that* job."

"Anybody home?" called a familiar voice from outside. Stevie shoved Magoo's head aside and peered into the stall.

Carole and Lisa pushed past the horse and let themselves out into the aisle. Fortunately, Magoo had finally calmed down a little and was standing quietly at the front of the stall, gazing at the newcomers.

"Look who I ran into on my way in," Stevie said. She gestured to Britt, who was standing beside her.

"Good," Lisa said. "Did you ask her yet?"

Stevie looked confused. "Ask her wh— Oh!" she exclaimed. "No, I totally forgot. I haven't been able to think about anything except how relieved I am that my grandma decided not to come today." She turned to Britt, who was stroking Magoo's nose. "Hey, Britt, we were hoping you'd be on our team for the gymkhana today." She gestured to include Carole and Lisa. "How about it?"

Britt's eyes widened. "Oh," she said softly.

Lisa smiled at her apologetically. "We've been meaning to ask you all week," she said. "Sorry to leave it to the last second like this. I hope you didn't think you wouldn't have a team to ride with."

113

"Um . . . ," Britt said. She paused, looking anxious. "Actually, I didn't. I mean, someone else already asked me to be on their team."

"Someone else?" Carole repeated. She exchanged puzzled glances with her friends. "What do you mean?"

Britt straightened Magoo's forelock and shrugged. "Polly asked me the other day," she said. "Lorraine and Anna are on the team, too."

Stevie could hardly believe her ears. "You mean you're already on somebody else's team for the gymkhana?" she asked.

"That's what she just said, Stevie," Lisa said, sounding a little testy. She turned to Britt and smiled. "Well, too bad for us," she said in a friendlier voice. "I hope your team does well. We'll see you later, okay?"

The three friends hurried away, leaving Britt with Magoo. As soon as they were out of earshot, Carole turned to her friends. "Can you believe that?" she asked. "Britt's already on a team!"

"Isn't it obvious what happened?" Lisa said. "Polly and her friends needed a fourth for their team, and they knew that Britt was new and a good rider. So they asked her, and she was too shy to turn them down. It's our fault for not asking her until now."

Stevie was nodding. "That makes perfect sense," she said. "We hadn't said anything to her yet about being teammates, and she was probably afraid to bring it up herself."

"And she didn't want to be left without a team," Carole finished. She sighed. "Boy, did we blow it this time."

Lisa looked grim. "No kidding," she said. She glanced at her watch. "The gymkhana starts in half an hour, and we still don't have a fourth person for our team."

Stevie gasped. "Oh no!" she said. "I didn't even think about that. We'd better hurry—let's split up and start asking people."

"DID YOU ASK Betsy?" Lisa asked. It was ten minutes later. The Saddle Club had just convened an emergency meeting in the aisle outside Magoo's stall. Britt had disappeared—probably to join up with her teammates—and the gelding was munching calmly on a mouthful of hay.

Carole nodded. "She and Meg are on a team with Joe and Adam."

"Of course," Stevie said. "It's not just a team, it's a double date." Betsy and Meg were each dating one of the boys.

"What about . . . um . . . ," Carole tried to think of another likely prospect.

"I asked everyone I saw," Lisa said bluntly. "Even all the younger kids turned us down."

"So did Simon," Stevie said. She patted Magoo as he stuck his head out of the stall and nudged her. "Can you believe he has a full team and we don't?" Simon Atherton was probably the worst rider in Horse Wise.

"What do we do now?" Carole asked. "Do you think Max will let us ride if we're short one person?"

The three girls were silent for a moment, pondering that question. That's when they heard heated words coming from the hallway around the corner from where they were standing.

"Some friends you are!" Veronica said, fuming. "Dumping me for some stupid boys!"

"Sorry, Veronica," Betsy's voice came. "We were sure you'd understand."

"But you didn't even tell me!" Veronica exclaimed angrily. "How am I supposed to find another team now? The gymkhana is starting in twenty minutes!"

"It was the boys' idea," Meg said apologetically. "They just suggested it last night when we were all at the movies—that's why we didn't tell you. We couldn't help saying yes when they asked us. It's so romantic."

Veronica let out a very unromantic-sounding snort. Then she came storming around the corner, almost barreling into The Saddle Club. "Watch where you're going," she spat out, not even seeming to realize how illogical her comment was, since they were standing still.

Lisa gulped and glanced at her friends, her heart sinking. They looked just as dismayed as she felt. But she knew what they had to do.

"Um, Veronica?" she said. "We couldn't help overhearing . . ."

* * *

"AT LEAST SHE'S a good rider," Carole said.

Lisa glanced at her. She and Carole were on their horses, watching Veronica and Stevie on the other side of the ring. Veronica took the loud, Hawaiian-print necktie that Stevie had just yanked off of Belle. The tie was already knotted, and Veronica slowly and carefully pulled it over Danny's head. "Would you stop saying that?" Lisa snapped at Carole. "Her riding skills don't help us much when she's so afraid of messing up her new manicure that she sabotages every single race."

"Go!" Stevie screamed as Veronica finally finished and remounted. The tie dangled from Danny's neck just below his head. It didn't seem to bother the horse one bit. "Canter! You've got to make up ground!"

But Veronica ignored Stevie's shouted commands and kept Danny to a sedate trot. Stevie urged Belle over toward her friends.

"Whose idea was it to give her the last lap in this race?" she fumed as Veronica crossed the finish line several yards behind the next-slowest rider, a six-year-old on a chubby pony.

"I don't think it would matter which lap she rode," Lisa pointed out logically. "She still would have slowed us down and made us lose. Just like she did in the last three games."

Despite her own anger at Veronica, Carole giggled. "I

guess we should consider ourselves lucky," she said. "It's a miracle we got Veronica to put that necktie on Danny at all. After all, it's not a designer original."

Lisa laughed at Carole's joke, but Stevie's face remained grim and angry. "She'd better shape up," she muttered. "I knew it wasn't going to be a pleasure having her on our team, but I thought we might at least have a chance of winning. Now, thanks to her stupid new hairdo and nail polish, we're practically in last place." Veronica had been to the beauty salon that morning with her mother and was afraid of messing up the results with too much hard riding. However, she hadn't mentioned that until *after* The Saddle Club had asked her to join their team.

"We never should have asked her," Stevie added, watching as Veronica rode slowly toward them. Max, Red, and Mrs. Reg were already busy removing the props from the costume race and setting up the ones for the next event.

Lisa shrugged. "We had to," she said. "Once Max found out we were short a team member and Veronica was short a team, he would have made us take her anyway."

Stevie knew that Lisa was right, but it didn't make her feel much better. "What's the big idea?" she demanded angrily when Veronica reached them. "We were in second place when I finished my lap. Thanks to you, we came in last."

Veronica raised one hand and examined her perfectly

rounded, bright red fingernails. "I thought I might have chipped a nail getting that hideous tie on Danny," she commented casually. "But it looks like I was lucky this time."

Stevie clenched her fists and gritted her teeth. She was trying to find the right words to tell Veronica exactly what she thought of her when Britt rode over to them.

"Hi," Britt said breathlessly. "That last race was fun, wasn't it?"

Veronica gave her a dismissive glance and snorted. Then she turned away, pulled a small compact mirror out of her pocket, and started checking the hair showing beneath her riding hat.

Britt gulped at Veronica's rudeness, then smiled bravely and continued. "I thought I'd never get those tube socks on over Coconut's hooves," she said to the other girls.

Stevie did her best to smile back despite her fury at Veronica. She and her friends wanted to be extra nice to Britt to prove to her that they really did like her, even though they hadn't asked her to be on their team until too late. Just because they weren't riding with Britt that day didn't mean she wasn't still an ideal Saddle Club member. "The tube socks were tough," she agreed.

"But they didn't seem to slow you down too much," Lisa added admiringly. She had ridden the same leg of the race as Britt and had been very impressed with her performance. *Just imagine if she were on our team*, Lisa thought wistfully. *Like she should be.*

"I know," Britt said, blushing but looking pleased. "I can hardly believe we won!" She glanced toward the small set of bleachers near the door, where two or three dozen spectators were watching the action. "Excuse me, I want to go say hi to my mom during the break," she said. "But I wanted to tell you that our snowball race is next."

Stevie grinned. "I know," she said. "It should be fun. Good luck."

"Good luck to you guys, too!" Britt called as she rode off toward the bleachers.

"So who's my partner for this stupid snowball thing?" Veronica asked, finally looking up from her nails.

Stevie sighed. Carole and Lisa had each already taken a turn paired with Veronica in previous events. "I guess that would be me," she muttered reluctantly.

The snowball race started well for The Saddle Club's team. According to the rules Stevie had devised, two members of each team had to ride across the ring keeping side by side but at least three feet apart. As they rode, the partners had to continually toss a snowball back and forth. If either partner dropped the snowball or held it for more than three seconds, he or she had to return to the beginning for a fresh snowball. When the first pair finished, the second pair from the team took their turn.

Carole and Lisa went in the first group. They managed to keep Starlight and Prancer trotting in perfect sync. Both were good enough riders to control their mounts without reins, which meant they could use both hands to catch the snowball. Neither of them dropped it, and they were in first place as they crossed the finish line and watched Stevie and Veronica move off.

For the first few strides, everything seemed to go well. Belle's and Danny's strides were well matched and even. Stevie tossed the snowball to Veronica. Veronica caught it easily and immediately lobbed it back. Stevie caught it. Back and forth, back and forth, the snowball sailed from one girl to the other.

Then, halfway across the ring, Stevie tossed the snowball once again. This time Veronica misjudged the throw, and her hand moved forward too quickly to meet it. The snowball bounced off the tips of her fingers and flew high into the air.

Carole clutched Starlight's mane anxiously as she watched. "Catch it!" she screamed. "You can still catch it!" Beside her, she was vaguely aware of Lisa screaming similar words.

Indeed, the snowball seemed to float lazily in the air as it arced above Danny's neck. All Veronica had to do was lean forward in the saddle and grab for it and all would be well. But she wasn't leaning forward. She wasn't even looking at the snowball any longer. She was staring at her own hand and frowning.

"My nail!" she wailed in dismay. "That stupid snowball bent it right back!"

The snowball seemed to fall in slow motion as Stevie watched in horror. Finally it landed in the dust of the ring floor with a splat. Meanwhile, people were cheering as Britt and Polly battled one other team for the lead. Veronica continued to peer at her broken nail, seemingly oblivious to anything else.

Stevie turned Belle and cantered back toward the cooler full of snowballs.

"Forget it, Stevie," Lisa called, riding over to meet her. "You'll never catch up now."

"I know," Stevie said as she dismounted and tossed Belle's reins to Carole, who had followed Lisa over. Then she started pulling all the leftover snowballs out of the cooler. "I'm not trying to win the race. I've got something else in mind for these."

Stevie smiled grimly as she stacked the last of the snowballs in the crook of her arm. She had had enough. It was time to teach Veronica a lesson.

Maybe a dozen snowballs down her back will convince her to try a little harder, Stevie thought. She ran back toward the center of the ring, where Veronica had dismounted and was picking at her jagged nail.

"Yoo-hoo!" Stevie said. "Veronica! I have something that might help." Before Veronica realized what was going on, Stevie had grabbed her by the shoulder.

But before she could start shoving snowballs down Veronica's shirt, Stevie happened to glance at the bleachers.

She paused in midmotion, hardly believing her eyes. Two people had just entered the ring and were taking seats in the front row.

One of them was Stevie's mother.

The other was Grandma Lake!

11

STEVIE DROPPED VERONICA'S shoulder immediately, gasping in horror.

"What's the big idea?" Veronica whined, rubbing her shoulder.

Stevie ignored her. She dropped the snowballs on the ground and raced back to her friends. "Look!" she whispered. "My grandma's here!"

Carole and Lisa turned to look at the bleachers. Stevie turned, too. When Grandma Lake saw them looking, she waved, smiling cheerfully. Stevie's mother waved, too.

Stevie returned their smile weakly and gave a quick wave. Then she turned back to her friends, biting her lip anxiously. "I've got to do something about this," she muttered.

124

"But what—" Lisa began. Then she stopped. Stevie had already raced away.

"What do you think she's going to do?" Carole asked.

Lisa shrugged and sighed. "Who knows?" she replied, gathering up Prancer's reins. Belle had turned to gaze after her mistress, and Lisa reached over to pat the mare. "But I can't really blame her for being worried."

Carole's glance strayed back to Stevie's grandmother. "Me neither," she said. "The gymkhana so far has been wild and crazy and exciting, just like always. That's good for us—well, most of us, anyway," she added as Veronica hurried past, filing busily at her fingernail with the emery board she had just pulled out of her jacket pocket.

"But bad for Grandma Lake," Lisa finished her friend's sentence.

Stevie was thinking the exact same thing as she grabbed Max by the arm. "Max!" she exclaimed breathlessly. "Which event is next?"

Max glanced down at the clipboard he was holding. "The shopping race," he said. He gestured to the far end of the ring, where Red was setting up the large signs Lisa had made. One read BLOOMINGDALE'S BRIDLES, another SAKS FIFTH AVENUE STIRRUPS, and so on. Nearby, Mrs. Reg was setting out the shopping bags at one station and the "merchandise" at another. According to the rules that Veronica had devised, each team would draw a receipt listing the names of items and stores. The riders would then have to locate their assigned items in the pile of merchandise, find the shopping bags with the correct store names, and drop them off at the corresponding store signs. Whoever delivered his or her items correctly and made it back over the finish line first was the winner.

Stevie thought fast. The shopping game was sure to be a wild scramble, with lots of excitement and thrills as the riders mounted and dismounted, scrabbled through the pile of items, grabbed at the shopping bags, and so on. She had to give Veronica at least a little bit of credit: Despite herself, the snobby girl had actually come up with a fun and wacky game. It was too bad that Stevie had to put a stop to it.

She tugged on Max's sleeve as he started to turn away. "Max," she said urgently. "Um, I think Veronica wanted to change the rules to the shopping game a little."

Max rolled his eyes. "It's a bit late for that," he said. "What does she want to do?"

"Well, first of all, she's worried about safety," Stevie said, "so she wants the riders to keep to a slow walk during the game."

For a moment Max seemed to be staring at something over Stevie's left shoulder. But then he returned his attention to her. "Oh, really?" he said, crossing his arms over his chest. "A walk, hmm? Anything else?"

"As a matter of fact, yes," Stevie said. She thought it was a good sign that Max was listening. Maybe she could still salvage this situation. "I think we should—um, I mean, *Veronica* thinks we should make the whole race less competitive. You know, concentrate more on cooperation." She smiled brightly. "Teamwork. Just like you're always teaching us in class. So instead of racing each other to return the stuff to the right store, the players should all help each other match things up. That way everybody wins."

Suddenly a loud, peevish voice came from just behind Stevie. "Hey, what's going on? You can't change the rules of my game, Stevie!"

Stevie whirled around to find Veronica standing there with her hands on her hips. She shot a desperate glance past Veronica toward the bleachers. How could she make Veronica—and more importantly, Max—understand how important it was to keep things calm from now on?

Veronica didn't give her a chance to come up with an argument. "My game stays exactly how I planned it," she said firmly, glaring at Max and then at Stevie. "Got it?"

"Okay, Veronica," Max said. "Calm down. Your game will go on as planned, don't worry. I'm sure Stevie's ideas were just suggestions."

Veronica tossed her head. "Well, they were stupid suggestions," she snapped. She turned on her heel and started to stomp away.

Unfortunately, Britt had chosen that moment to approach. She tried to jump aside, but Veronica was moving too fast. The two girls slammed into each other—hard.

Veronica had momentum on her side and managed to keep her feet. Britt went flying, ending up on her backside in the dirt.

"Oh!" she exclaimed. She was blinking hard, obviously trying to hold back tears. "I'm sorry, I—"

Veronica didn't let her finish. "I thought I told you to watch where you're going!" she screamed at the top of her lungs. A hush fell over the ring as everyone turned to see what the commotion was about. Veronica glared down at Britt, who was still on the ground. "You're always getting in my way! Someone as clumsy as you are shouldn't even be allowed near horses!"

Britt was blinking faster, but she didn't say anything. She just sat still where she had fallen, her face turning red.

Stevie didn't say anything, either. But she didn't stay still. She couldn't. Britt might not be a full-fledged member of The Saddle Club yet, but that didn't matter. Even if she had been a total stranger, Stevie couldn't have let this pass. Especially not after the way Veronica had been acting all during the gymkhana.

Stevie turned and raced back to the center of the ring, where the snowballs she had dropped had started to melt in the warmth of the stable. Several of them had begun to merge, forming a large, icy blob. She grabbed the blob. The bottom of it was coated with a thick layer of dirt, sawdust, grit, and straw, which was clinging to the frozen mass.

128

Seconds later, Stevie had returned to the scene of the incident. Britt still hadn't moved. Neither had anyone else. Max seemed too stunned to respond, and nobody else seemed sure what to do. Out of the corner of her eye, Stevie saw Ms. Lynn start to rise from her seat.

Veronica alone seemed unperturbed by her own obnoxious behavior. She turned away from Britt and carefully rearranged her riding hard hat, which had been knocked slightly askew in the collision.

Stevie strode up to her. "Oh, Veronica," she said in a singsong voice.

Veronica looked up, an irritated expression on her face. "What do you want?"

Stevie grinned and held up the grimy snow blob. It was too big to shove down Veronica's shirt. She shoved it in her face instead. "This is what Britt and I think of your obnoxious behavior," she said, knocking off Veronica's hat and rubbing the dirty slush into her expensively cut hair.

Veronica shrieked in dismay. Britt gasped in surprise. Max looked uncertain whether to start yelling or laughing. And from the direction of the bleachers came a hoot and then the sound of applause. "All right, Stevie!" someone yelled.

Stevie glanced over, expecting to see Ms. Lynn leading the cheers. Ms. Lynn was clapping, all right. But the one standing on the bleacher seat, hooting and hollering and grinning from ear to ear, was Grandma Lake.

* * *

STEVIE WAS SO stunned by her grandmother's behavior that she hardly heard Veronica apologize to Britt at Max's stern command. She barely saw Veronica stomp off, face dripping with filthy melted snow, in the direction of the bathroom, or return a few minutes later with wet but clean hair and a freshly scrubbed face. She might not even have noticed when the shopping game started if Carole and Lisa hadn't come over with Belle, shoved a receipt into her hand, and helped her to mount.

The players lined up, and Stevie glanced down at her receipt. "Wait!" she cried when she finally snapped back to awareness of her surroundings. "We've got to keep to a walk during this game. Did everyone hear me? Don't go any faster than a walk!"

Everybody ignored her. As soon as Mrs. Reg gave the command, all the players rode pell-mell toward the pile of shopping bags.

Stevie followed, her heart in her throat. What had she done? Not only had she failed to convince Max to keep the gymkhana calm, but she had caused a big ruckus herself and gotten her grandmother all worked up. Why did Veronica have to be such a jerk? And why couldn't she, Stevie, contain herself and plan some suitably humiliating revenge for sometime when Grandma Lake wasn't around?

Still, Stevie told herself as she dismounted and grabbed the Bloomingdale's shopping bag from the pile, it had *almost* been worth it to smash that dirty, disgusting pile of slush into Veronica's obnoxious face.

She shook her head. What was she thinking? It hadn't been worth it at all. Getting revenge on Veronica was a million times less important than protecting her grandmother's health.

Stevie was so distracted by her thoughts that she came in last in the shopping race. Next came the backward obstacle course, and once again Stevie tried to convince Max to tone down the excitement.

Once again, he refused. "Don't be ridiculous, Stevie," he said. "The whole point is riding backward. The course is too easy if you ride forward. It wouldn't be a challenge at all."

That didn't sound like a problem to Stevie. No challenge meant no excitement, and no excitement meant no problem for her grandmother. But Max stood firm. As the race started, Stevie crossed her fingers for luck. Just in case that failed, she also started trying to figure out the best way to tell her father that she had been responsible for his mother's heart attack.

"I THINK WE set a new record out there today," Carole said ruefully as she led Starlight out of the ring.

Lisa was right behind her with Prancer. "You mean for having the lowest team score in gymkhana history?" The award ceremony had ended a few minutes earlier. The Saddle Club's team had come in dead last. Carole and

Lisa had walked their horses at one end of the ring to cool them off after all of the exercise, and now Starlight and Prancer were ready to return to their stalls.

Stevie joined her friends just in time to hear their comments. "I'm sorry, guys," she said morosely. "I know I wasn't exactly performing my best out there. I guess I was a little distracted."

"It's okay," Lisa said sympathetically. "We know you were worried about your grandma. Besides, Veronica was so grumpy after you humiliated her that she did even worse than you."

Carole giggled. "Boy, was she mad," she said. But when she saw Stevie's face, she stopped laughing immediately. "Don't worry, Stevie," she said. "I'm sure your grandmother is fine. Where is she now? Did you check on her?" When Stevie hadn't joined them while they were cooling down the horses, the other two girls had assumed that she was with her grandmother.

"I tried," Stevie replied. "But on my way to the bleachers, Ms. Lynn stopped me to thank me for sticking up for Britt. By the time I got over to where my mom and grandma had been sitting, they were gone." She let out a heavy sigh. "They're probably rushing to the emergency room for some oxygen or something."

Lisa was pretty sure that that wasn't the case. Grandma Lake hadn't looked all that frail to her when the older woman was stomping on the bleachers and cheering at the top of her lungs. But she knew Stevie too well to say so. Stevie wasn't going to stop worrying until she saw for herself that her grandmother was still alive and well.

"Come on, let's get these guys put away," Carole said, gesturing at the horses.

Stevie nodded and patted Belle on the neck. "They all did their best, even if we can't say the same for their riders," she muttered.

Lisa gave her a comforting look. "Don't worry about it, Stevie," she said. "Now come on. We've still got to go check on Magoo when we're done with our horses. After that, maybe we could go to TD's for a quick snack. A nice butterscotch swirl, lime sherbet, and marshmallow sundae is sure to make you feel better, right?"

Stevie shrugged. "I doubt it," she said glumly. "But I might as well go with you. I'm in no hurry to get home and face the bad news."

The Saddle Club met up again in front of Magoo's stall a few minutes later. The gelding had left his bandages alone for a change, and it didn't take the girls long to check on him. As they were carefully grooming around his injuries, Britt stopped by the stall.

"Oh!" Carole said when she saw her. "Hi. How are you?" She wondered if Britt was still upset by her unpleasant encounter with Veronica.

Britt grinned, not looking upset at all. "Great," she said, pointing to the blue ribbon clipped to her belt. Her team had come in first place in the gymkhana.

"Congratulations," Lisa said with a smile. She held the

stall door open so that The Saddle Club could join Britt in the aisle. "Did you have fun?"

"Definitely," Britt assured her. She gave Stevie a sidelong glance, then stared down at her shoes. "Um, by the way, thanks for sticking up for me back there," she said softly. "It was really nice of you."

"You're welcome," Stevie said. "You know, you shouldn't be too intimidated by Veronica. Her bark is much worse than her bite."

Britt looked up and smiled. "I know that now," she said bashfully. "Thanks to you."

Britt seemed embarrassed by the whole topic, so Carole decided to change it. "Hey, Britt," she said cheerfully. "We were just about to head over to TD's for a snack. Do you want to join us?"

"Thanks," Britt said. "That's really nice of you to ask. But actually, my teammates and I were planning to go there together and celebrate." She paused, looking uncertain. "Um, I'm sure Polly and the others wouldn't mind if you guys came with us . . ."

"No, no, that's okay," Stevie assured her quickly, perking up a little at the mention of Polly's name. Maybe Britt was so eager to go out with Polly because she was interested in Romeo's half brother! Stevie didn't want to discourage that. "You go ahead." It would be wonderful if Britt actually ended up buying the horse that Stevie had chosen for her. With all the bad things that had happened that day, Stevie couldn't resist prying just a little in hopes of finding a nugget of good news. "Um, by the way, you never really told us what you thought of that horse Polly took you to see," she said, trying to sound casual. "Did you like him? Polly didn't try to talk you into buying him or anything, did she?"

Britt smiled and glanced around to make sure nobody else was around. "Actually, now that you mention it," she said, "I just found out something wonderful. Can you keep a secret?"

Stevie, Carole, and Lisa nodded, exchanging glances. Britt's face was positively glowing. Whatever her news was, it must be really good. And unless they missed their guess, that meant that Britt had picked out her next horse. Which one had she chosen?

Stevie tried to control her grin. She was sure it was Romeo's brother. After all, that's the horse they had been discussing when Britt had brought it up. And why else would the new girl be hanging around with Polly so much?

Carole was of a different opinion. Britt and Coconut had performed brilliantly together in the gymkhana. They made a wonderful team—that was probably what had made up the girl's mind.

Meanwhile, Lisa was crossing her fingers and hoping that Applesauce was the horse the new girl was talking about. True, Britt had done well on Coconut. But the gymkhana games had been demanding. Maybe she had missed the mare's cool and professional response to her every command. Maybe she had just realized how perfect Applesauce would have been in the gymkhana.

"Polly convinced me to ask my mom, and she said yes!" Britt said, looking even more ecstatic. She turned toward the stall behind them and broke into a full-fledged grin. "She's going to buy Magoo for me!"

"Magoo?" the three members of The Saddle Club repeated in a single, astonished voice.

"You're buying Magoo?" Carole added in disbelief.

Britt nodded and reached up to stroke the horse's long nose. "Can you believe it?" she said happily. "I didn't think we could afford it right now. But Mom said it was no problem. It's so great—Magoo is the perfect horse for me!"

Just then, Polly appeared at the end of the aisle and waved at Britt. Britt waved in reply, then turned back to The Saddle Club, looking anxious. "I guess they're ready to go," she said. "I was going to offer to help with Magoo, but—"

"Don't worry," Stevie said. "Go ahead. We'll finish up here today." She grinned weakly. "But starting tomorrow, he's all yours."

Britt beamed. "It's a deal!" She hurried to join Polly, pausing only long enough to give Magoo a kiss on the nose and The Saddle Club a brief wave.

Lisa watched her go, stunned. "Did I just hear what I thought I heard?" she asked. "She actually wants to buy . . . Magoo?"

136

All three girls turned to stare at the horse for a long moment. Magoo stared back impassively, chewing on a mouthful of hay he'd just pulled from his hayrack.

"But he's so fussy," Carole said at last, breaking their mystified silence.

"And fidgety," Stevie added.

"And fearful," Lisa said. "And demanding and nervous and everything else you could think of." She let out a bewildered sigh. "Still, Britt's been helping us deal with him all along. She must know what she's getting into, right?"

Before her friends could answer, they heard someone calling their names. They looked up and saw Ms. Lynn hurrying down the aisle toward them. "Hello, girls," she said when she reached them. "Have you seen Britt?"

"She just left," Lisa said. "She was going over to TD's with her teammates. You might be able to catch her if you—"

"No, no," Ms. Lynn interrupted. "That's okay. I didn't realize she'd already left." She smiled. "Isn't it wonderful that she's already made friends as nice as Polly, Anna, and Lorraine? Anyway, I was just hoping to get a look at this horse she's fallen in love with. Could you show me which stall Magoo is in?"

Stevie stepped aside and gestured at the gelding behind her. "No problem," she said. "He's right here."

Ms. Lynn stepped closer and took a good look at Magoo. "Oh my," she said. "He really does seem to have some recovering to do. No wonder Max was so careful about letting her ride him."

"Britt has ridden Magoo?" Lisa asked. She glanced at her friends, who looked just as surprised as she was.

"Well of course," Ms. Lynn said, still watching the horse. "My Britt wouldn't decide to buy a horse she'd never ridden." She smiled and patted Magoo on the nose. "Although it would have been a real shame if her test ride hadn't worked out. Magoo sounds like such an ideal choice for her."

The Saddle Club glanced at one another again. "Um, how do you mean, exactly?" Carole asked cautiously. "I mean, don't get me wrong. Magoo is a perfectly fine horse in some ways. But he is a little, well . . ." She searched her mind for the most tactful word. ". . . demanding."

Ms. Lynn laughed and turned away from the horse to face the girls. "Oh, but that's what makes him so perfect!" she exclaimed. Her eyes twinkled. "Britt's old horse back in Ohio was a real fussbudget, too. Magoo doesn't look anything like him, but it sounds like their personalities are practically an exact match. That's what Britt likes best—fussing over a fussy horse."

"Really?" Stevie said. "But she's so shy and everything, so we thought—"

Ms. Lynn was already nodding understandingly. "I know," she said. "You thought Britt needed a horse that could take care of her, not the other way around." She shrugged. "I really should have explained before I asked you to help me find her a horse. I just didn't think about it, I suppose—although you still managed to help her find her dream horse." She turned to pat Magoo again. "You see, taking care of an animal that's needy and insecure brings out the best and boldest in Britt's own personality." She smiled. "I think you may notice a real change in Britt now that she has Magoo." She glanced around to make sure that nobody else was around, then winked conspiratorially. "And I think that girl Veronica will notice, too. She'd better watch out. Britt may not be very good at defending herself, but when it comes to her horse . . ."

The three girls nodded. All of them were too speechless to respond otherwise. Was Ms. Lynn really talking about the same Britt they knew?

"Well," Ms. Lynn said, giving Magoo one final pat, "I'd better get going. But thanks again, all of you—for everything." She hurried away.

Carole was the first to speak. "Wow," she said. "I guess we really misjudged Britt's taste in horses."

"That's not all we misjudged about her," Lisa pointed out. "We also misjudged her intentions."

Stevie leaned against the door of the stall across from Magoo's. "What do you mean?" she asked. "Her intentions about what?"

"About being our friend," Lisa said. "I mean, I'm sure she likes us just fine, but it's obvious now that she wasn't hanging around us so much because she was trying to be our new best friend." She shrugged. "She was getting to know Magoo."

Stevie nodded slowly. "Now that I think about it," she said, "she did mostly show up when we were here at his stall. And she was always willing to help out with his care—even when she begged off other things, like making props for the gymkhana."

As usual, Carole was still more interested in the part of their discussion having to do with horses. "I still can't believe how wrong we were," she said. "I really thought Britt would be happiest with a horse that was the opposite of herself—like Coconut, or Applesauce, or Romeo's brother—to help her out of her shell."

"But what she really needs is a horse that will force her to take the lead," Lisa said. "Who could have guessed?"

Stevie sighed. "People really aren't always what they seem, are they?" she said. As soon as the words were out of her mouth, she gasped and suddenly stood up straight. "Oh my gosh!" she exclaimed.

"What is it?" Lisa asked.

Stevie was already hurrying down the aisle toward the entryway. "Sorry," she called back over her shoulder, "I can't make it to TD's after all. I've got to get home. I'll explain later."

Before her friends could ask any more questions, she had disappeared around the corner at the end of the aisle.

Carole looked at Lisa and shrugged. "I wonder what that was all about?" she said.

"I don't know," Lisa replied. She turned as Magoo let out an irritable snort from behind them. "Maybe this is just her way of getting out of the rest of Magoo's grooming."

Carole smiled and headed for the stall door to finish their interrupted task. "That's okay," she said. "I don't mind doing it one more time, now that we know that he'll be Britt's problem from now on."

As soon as Stevie arrived home, she went in search of her grandmother. It didn't take long to find her. Grandma Lake was sitting at the kitchen table, bent over a crossword puzzle.

She looked up when Stevie entered. "Oh, hello, dear," she said. "We didn't expect you back from the stable so soon. Your mother and father just ran to the grocery store." She smiled and set down her pencil. "By the way, you were wrong about your show today being boring. It was a lot of fun!"

Stevie gulped in a deep lungful of air. She had run all the way home and was out of breath, but she didn't want to waste a second getting it back. She had too much to say. "I'm sorry, Grandma," she gasped.

Grandma Lake looked surprised. She pulled out the chair beside her and patted the seat. "Sit down, Stevie," she said. "You look worn out. Now, what's all this about being sorry?"

Stevie collapsed into the chair and leaned wearily on the table. "I knew the gymkhana would be fun," she explained. "I tried to keep you away because I thought . . . um . . ." Now that she was here, she wasn't sure how to explain things. "Well, I thought it might be too much for you."

Luckily, her grandmother caught on quickly. "Too much for me? You thought it might be too much for me?" she said. She sat back in her chair, looking thunderstruck. "So *that's* what's wrong with this place!" she exclaimed.

"What do you mean?" Stevie asked.

Grandma Lake leaned forward again and laughed. She reached out and smoothed back Stevie's dark blond hair, which was sticking out all over the place from her run. "I thought maybe it was just because you kids were getting older and more mature," she said. "That seemed like the only explanation for why this house seemed so much, well, *duller* than I remembered it." Seeing Stevie's surprised expression, she laughed again. "Sorry, I guess that's not very tactful. But I must say, I was quite disappointed. My favorite thing about coming to this house back when you were younger was all the wonderful chaos and excitement. You kids were always so rambunctious, playing all sorts of pranks on one another."

Stevie's mind was slowly digesting all this. "But we thought maybe you wouldn't be able to handle that kind of thing," she said. "I mean, Mom and Dad yelled at us about behaving better right before you came. And then when you got off the plane you seemed so tired . . ."

Grandma Lake chuckled. "I *was* tired that night," she said. "For one thing, the plane was late, and I'd been sitting in that narrow seat far too long for comfort. Besides, I had played in a tennis tournament that afternoon just before I left for the airport." She grinned proudly. "I won, too."

Stevie was starting to see things much more clearly now. Playing tennis and cheering at a gymkhana matched her hazy memories of Grandma Lake much better than sipping tea and puttering around dusty museums. That reminded her. "What about at the art museum?" she said. "You kept yawning there. I thought all that walking wore you out."

"Nope," Grandma Lake replied, still grinning. "Actually, I didn't yawn half as much as you did—I saw you, even though you tried to hide it. And we were both yawning for the same reason. We were bored stiff." She shook her head. "May I never get so old that I actually enjoy hanging out in dingy old museums."

Stevie shook her head, too, amazed that she could have misunderstood her grandmother so completely. But she was glad that she had finally figured out that Grandma Lake might not be as feeble as she and her brothers had thought. It was her own comment about misjudging Britt that had made her realize it. "So this means we acted different because we thought you were too old," she said. "And you thought we were acting different because *we* were too old."

Not many people would have been able to follow that logic, but Grandma Lake had no trouble at all. "Exactly," she said.

Stevie knew she would have to find her brothers and tell them about this. But first, she had one more thing to say to Grandma Lake. "I'm sorry," she said, grabbing her grandmother by both hands and squeezing tight. "I feel terrible. Here we thought we were helping keep you safe and healthy, when in fact we were practically boring you to death! Can you forgive me?"

Her grandmother pretended to think about it for a minute. Then she smiled. "I suppose so," she said. "As long as you promise to remember that a true Lake *never* prefers things dull and safe." She extricated her hands from Stevie's grasp and leaned over to give her a hug. "And you've got another week to help make it up to me by keeping this place lively. I expect you to show me a good time for the next six days—Lake style."

Stevie laughed with delight. "Great!" she exclaimed. "We can start by putting our heads together and figuring out the perfect way to get back at Alex for hiding my riding boots in the fireplace!"

12

"WHAT ARE YOU looking at?" Stevie asked the next Saturday as she rode Belle over to join her friends, who were waiting for her just outside the stable. It was a cool but sunny winter day, and The Saddle Club had decided to take a leisurely trail ride after their unmounted Horse Wise meeting.

Lisa gathered up her reins more firmly. Prancer was feeling frisky, and she didn't want to lose control of the mare. "Britt and Polly," she said. "They were heading for the southwest trails. I guess they had the same idea we did."

"Can you believe how much time those two have been spending together this week?" Carole added, gazing across the fields at the spot where the two riders had just disappeared into the woods. "They're inseparable at school, too. I can't believe it took us so long to notice that they were becoming best friends."

Stevie nodded and signaled to Belle for a trot. "Come on," she called over her shoulder. "Let's head north. I'd rather not bump into them."

Carole giggled. "Why not?" she teased, urging Starlight into a brisk trot as well. "Are you afraid Polly will think we're trying to steal her new friend away?"

Stevie shook her head as the three friends rode side by side toward the woods north of Pine Hollow. The girls had spent a lot of time over the past week discussing Britt's friendship with Polly, but Stevie still couldn't believe the way it had snuck up on them all. "I did notice that Britt and Polly seemed to be together a lot the week before the gymkhana," she said, "but I thought it was because of Romeo's half brother."

"I didn't notice anything at all," Lisa admitted, and Carole nodded in agreement.

The girls rode silently for a few minutes, each thinking her own thoughts. The horses moved easily, obviously enjoying the exercise.

The girls slowed their mounts to a walk as they entered the woods. "Still," Carole said, breaking the silence, "I guess it all worked out for the best. Britt and Polly are both happy. And Magoo looks great."

"Isn't it amazing?" Lisa said. "I can't believe he's

healthy enough to ride already, but Judy okayed him days ago. I guess now that Britt is nursing him full-time, he finally wants to get better."

"You're not kidding when you say she's nursing him *full-time*," Stevie said, zipping her jacket up a little tighter in the chilliness of the shady path. "She spends even more time at the stable than we do."

Carole grinned. "And that's no easy task," she said. "By the way, now that Magoo's attitude has improved, I've got to admit it: I think we underestimated him. I saw Britt taking him over a few jumps yesterday after school, and he's got real talent."

"Who would have guessed it?" Lisa commented.

"Not me," Carole said. "That's probably partly because we only knew him when he was injured. But I also thought that he wasted too much energy fussing and fretting to be any good in the ring."

"Maybe Britt can help him channel that energy," Lisa said. "If anyone can do it, she can."

Stevie nodded. "She really does know what she's doing," she said a bit grudgingly. "And she's totally horse-crazy. It's too bad she didn't turn out to be Saddle Club material after all."

Lisa turned to look at her friend, who was riding beside her on the wide, smooth trail. "I don't know about that, Stevie," she said. "Just because Britt isn't a member of The Saddle Club, that doesn't mean she can't still be our friend."

"Right," Carole said. "She's just *better* friends with Polly, that's all. And that's fine, right?"

"Right," Lisa agreed.

Stevie shrugged. "Okay, I guess you're right," she said. She looked thoughtful for a moment. "It's been an interesting few weeks, hasn't it?"

"That's for sure," Carole said. Suddenly she realized what Stevie was probably thinking about. "Oh! That reminds me. We never asked you if your grandmother made it home all right."

"Safe and sound," Stevie said. "Actually, she called this morning to tell us she made friends with the man sitting next to her on the plane last night. He wants to take her dancing next weekend." She grinned. "He's about ten years younger than she is. But she's pretty sure he can keep up with her—he looks nice and strong and healthy."

Her friends laughed. "It's great that your grandma turned out to be so much fun," Lisa said.

"She sure did," Stevie said, guiding Belle around a large rock in the trail. "We had a blast at Busch Gardens last Sunday. She went on the roller coaster with me about ten times, even after my brothers were all too dizzy. I hope I have that much energy when I'm her age." She smiled at the memory of the day at the amusement park. Alex had been positively green around the gills after his third spin on the roller coaster—mostly because Grandma Lake, at

Stevie's urging, had dared him to eat *four* chili dogs and a banana split for lunch. That would teach him to hide her boots! "I'm just sorry I wasted a whole week treating her like an invalid," Stevie added. "I should have figured things out sooner. Mrs. Reg did, remember?"

Lisa gasped. She had almost forgotten about Mrs. Reg's story. "So that's what she was talking about," she said. "Your grandma. I thought the story had something to do with Magoo."

"Maybe it did," Carole pointed out, "whether she meant it to or not. Stevie may have misjudged her grandmother, but we kind of misjudged Magoo, too."

"Among other things," Stevie said, thinking of Britt and Polly.

"Well, I guess things are finally getting back to normal now," Lisa said. She ducked her head as Prancer walked under a low-hanging branch. "School has started again . . ."

"We don't have to take care of Magoo anymore," Carole added. "But he's a full-time resident of Pine Hollow now, instead of just a guest."

"So is Britt," Lisa said. Until this week, Britt had been coming to Pine Hollow on a trial basis. But now she was a permanent member of Horse Wise and The Saddle Club's riding class.

"Things are back to normal at my house, too," Stevie said. "Well, normal for us, anyway."

Carole grinned. "And Veronica is still mad at us—especially Stevie—about what happened at the gymkhana. That's normal, too."

"And here we are, just the three of us, on a trail ride together," Stevie said, leaning forward to give her horse a pat on the neck. She looked over at the other two founding members of The Saddle Club and smiled. "Totally normal. Maybe it's not exactly what we would have predicted a week or two ago," she added contentedly, "but right now, being back to normal feels awfully good to me."

ABOUT THE AUTHOR

Bonnie Bryant is the author of nearly a hundred books about horses, including The Saddle Club series, Saddle Club Supers, and the Pony Tails series. She has also written novels and movie novelizations under her married name, B. B. Hiller.

Ms. Bryant began writing The Saddle Club in 1986. Although she had done some riding before that, she intensified her studies then and found herself learning right along with her characters Stevie, Carole, and Lisa. She claims that they are all much better riders than she is.

Ms. Bryant was born and raised in New York City. She still lives there, in Greenwich Village, with her two sons.

Don't miss Bonnie Bryant's next exciting
Saddle Club adventure . . .

HORSE WHISPERS
The Saddle Club #74

The Saddle Club is spending February vacation with
the Devines at the Bar None Ranch. Colonel Devine
has just bought some new horses, and one of the
mares reminds Carole of Cobalt, the first horse she
really loved. Carole rides the mare and discovers that
although the mare has been trained, there is still
something wild in her.

Then the mare disappears, and The Saddle Club
and Kate Devine have to find her. When they do,
they have a tough decision to make. Will they be able
to bring themselves to give her the freedom she
wants? Or will they find a way to make her give up the
wild life? And what can the mare teach Carole about
herself? Is there more than one way for horse and rider
to communicate?